YEAR

Zoha Kazemi

YEAR OF THE TREE

Translated by
Caroline Croskery

Printed by CreateSpace
An Amazon.com Company
CreateSpace, Charleston, SC USA

First Edition, 2016.
Printed by CreateSpace

eStore address: https://www.createspace.com/6527926

Available from Amazon.com and other retail outlets
Available on Kindle and other devices

ISBN-13: 978-1537308630
ISBN-10: 1537308637

Printed in the United States of America

Table of Contents

Family Tree

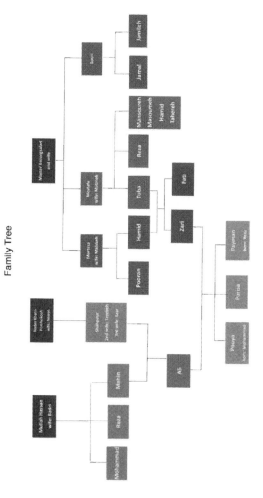

One

A vibration rattles the window panes. Loud music reverberates off the walls of the house, seeming near and then far from you. The room gets smaller and then larger. The door is shaking intensely, both from the pulsating drum in the loud music and from Parisa beating on it. You turn it up but you still hear Parisa screaming over the music. You don't answer her. You sway your wide back over your short, fat legs. Your arms swirl in the air and through your almond-shaped eyes, you see your Mom, who arrives along with the guests. You twist and move your plump body. Parisa bangs on the door again, demanding that you turn it off. She begs you to open the door. She has already told you that they would be coming to see the house. But you don't care. It is time to dance now.

In her green, three-quarter sleeve blouse and black wool skirt, Mom stands there clapping for you with her usual smile. The harder Parisa pounds on the door, the higher you turn the music up. You turn it all the way up.

She isn't pounding on the door now. She has given up and gone away. You are glad. You walk over to your desk and pick up Mrs. Smith's picture. Mrs. Smith takes your short, fat fingers and rises from her chair. You push aside the wedding veil from her face and stroke her long, chestnut hair. You give the signal. She begins to dance as she raises her long arms above her head and turns a pirouette against your short arms. Mom claps as you turn one too.

Pooya, you are the only person who knows that sadness and happiness have nothing to do with each other. Happiness is a time to be joyful and forget one's troubles. It can happen at any time, even in the most sorrowful of times, in the most intense moments of melancholy, in the most devastating times of grief. Like the time when Parisa and Dad tried to make you understand that   I was gone, and the house was filled with mourners who had come to offer their condolences for my early demise, when you stubbornly walked past my portrait with the black ribbon around it and remembered the last image you had of me, an image red from the blood and white from the paleness caused by my pain. You walked right past, and saw the pain in your Mom's absent face, in the tears of Tooba's vacant eyes, in the brokenness of your Dad's back, in Parisa's burning heart. You found refuge in your room, in the loud music and your love for Mrs. Smith. You would never understand my absence as you never have understood; for you there is no difference between happiness and sadness. They have nothing to do with each other.

The room is full of guests. They all clap and whistle. Dad is there too, sitting off to the side among the guests. You walk toward him to give him a kiss. He gets up and walks over to you passing the men and women sitting in the room. He is smiling. He has shaved off his beard and put on a red tie. You stroke your face to feel how the stubbles of whiskers have grown. You loved the red ties that dad used to fasten for you even though the tie looked ugly around your short, fat neck connecting your baldish head to your narrow shoulders. But we said that it looked great on you. And you would say, "I I I h h hope I I I will b b be a gr r room soon." And we would all laugh gleefully.

I am not among your guests. You never invite me anymore. Ever since that day, you don't like seeing your little brother in the afternoon. That one time was enough. I wish you could have seen me like I was before. The old Payman who wasn't injured. The Payman who was healthy and on his feet. I wish you could wipe from your mind my blood-splattered image. You haven't seen me for a year since my death. Just once. That day that Parisa said her visa was ready and bought her ticket. You became ill. That afternoon, by the time I joined the guests you entertained in your mind, you were so frightened that

11

you fainted right on the spot. When Parisa noticed through the deafening music blasting through the crack in the door to your room, that you weren't clapping or whistling no matter how hard she pounded on the door and listened, she couldn't hear you, she had no choice but to call Mr. Safa to break the door down. Your blood pressure was under nine. I left you spending one night in the hospital. Even though, you generally don't mind – you like the atmosphere in the hospital, doctors, and getting shots. You love getting all that attention and making everyone worry about you. And you play innocent as much as you can. You didn't remember what you had seen or why your wedding fell through.

Aunt Fati had also come to the hospital and was doting upon you. You didn't like seeing her. I understand. She looks like Mom, but not enough for you to make such a fuss over it. You screamed. She didn't stay. She left. After Mom, you couldn't see her. Parisa politely asked her to leave. You asked Parisa for water. And as you sat there on your bed, you raised your head and sipped the water from the glass Parisa held for you. Then you took her hand and kissed it. Parisa kissed you on the forehead. You didn't see the tears she wiped off her cheeks as she left the emergency room, or her sniffling. But actually, you did hear it.

All of a sudden the loud music stops. It is dead quiet. The light goes off. The guests are shocked. You hear Parisa's footsteps walking in long, firm strides towards your door. She knocks but you have locked your door so that she wouldn't be able to come in. You neither open the door nor answer her. Parisa yells that you have forced her to cut the fuse. She is angry and yelling at you. You don't understand why. Why would she be screaming instead of dancing? She knocks, but you stay put in your place. She yells, she screams, "Open the door!" But you don't want to hear it. Instead, you go to the window and throw back the curtains to light up the room. And you hear Parisa again, "I'll be rid of you in just a few more days!" Why? What have you done? You stand there in the middle of your room. "Open the door! They'll be here any minute! Open the door right now! What does your room look like? What are you wearing?"

You look down at yourself. You are wearing pajama pants and an old t-shirt. You stroke your face. It is stubbly and rough. Mrs. Smith might not like that. No groom has stubble on his wedding night. You have to take a shower. If Parisa finds out, she won't like it. Right now is no time to take a shower. She has told you many times, "Don't go and take a shower when we have guests." Because sometimes you forget and come walking out of the shower all the way to your room with only a towel wrapped around you. This situation upsets everybody but you don't understand why.

Parisa is still yelling. You sense crying in her voice. But you don't answer. Parisa threatens you that she will go and if you don't open the door and come out, she won't turn the power back on or serve you your dinner. You know she's just bluffing. She is always angry at first, but then later becomes nicer. You don't want to upset your little sister. Especially since she has tried so hard to fill Mom's shoes after Mom's death. She has tried to be a Mom to you as well as a sister, even though she knows well that she has not been able to do so. You know it too. You feel her inability with your whole being. You don't want to throw it back at her. You know she is trying. But in any case, it's not in your hands. When it gets to this point, it's like the inner Pooya wakes up. The Pooya who wants to keep going to the end even if it means missing meals. This other Pooya gets your clothes ready; he gets out a t-shirt, jeans and clean underwear from your drawer and folds them neatly on your bed. He takes your razor into the shower. The other Pooya, like you, isn't afraid of the dark. But he doesn't know how to take a shower in the dark.

You wait awhile. You wait patiently for the guests to appear one by one to shake your hand as they say goodbye. You know that Parisa will ultimately connect the fuse. She has to. She's waiting for the doorbell to ring. Your bedroom, the shower and bathroom, the living room and the entrance hallway are all on the same fuse. Also the doorbell. The room lights up and the deafening music fills the room. You quickly turn off the music and go towards the shower. There are boxes everywhere – outside the bedroom doors, in the halls, in the kitchen and living room. Parisa has given you three boxes and a suitcase to pack up all your things in. You don't understand why. You don't know where you will be going. You don't know that Parisa is up all night crying and that is why she is irritable and nags all day long – because she is so tired. Because making decisions these days has been so painful for her. Well, she has no choice, poor thing. She has to think of the future. Of course, you haven't yet lifted a finger. Don't worry. She'll finally pack your things too and so that you won't have a fit while she does it, she'll do it at night while you are fast asleep.

She puts your clothes and personal belongings in the suitcase and the rest in boxes. She is going to put the boxes in Aunt Fati's basement. She is going to try to throw away, give away and sell as many things as she can. She puts the stereo in a box. She tells you a lie that you can take it with you. You can't. It's not allowed. Instead, she hides your photograph of Angelina Jolie, Mrs. Smith, in your clothes along with a few CD's that you really like in the hopes that they have a CD player there so that you can play them and dance whenever you like. Well, they surely have a CD player. Don't worry about it. You'll be able to hear music and dance twice a week. All the dormitories have community rooms where they hold gatherings and celebrations. On Friday and Monday afternoons you'll have live music too. Uncle Keyvan will play the keyboard for you and you'll dance. The same goes for birthdays. You'll have lots of parties to go to. Don't worry.

There you make friends with Mehdi. You both look at pictures. Mehdi falls in love with your Mrs. Smith.

You teach him all about love. You eat together, fight with each other and then make up. You both hope to get married. You go over your wedding plans with each other and the list of people you plan to invite from the institution. You also invite Parisa. You tell him about Parisa and Mehdi tells you about his elderly grandmother.

They give injections to you both, every so often. Of course, it doesn't matter to you. Parisa knows about it and she knows that there is no choice in the matter. Each one of you, if you want to implement your wedding plans, the moment when you can't control yourself might make things worse. Mr. Mollaei has explained this issue to Parisa and Parisa has signed the consent form.

Well, sometimes you feel down and you cry. Each time you have a bout of weeping behind your closed doors, it causes more strands of Parisa's hair to turn grey. Parisa stands by your door and cries with you, even though she knows you will feel better and calm down afterwards. But they don't know this at the institution. She has told them everything, except for this. She completely forgot to explain it.

They will be worried at first. Mr. Mostafavi, the on-call nurse would try to come into your room to calm you down. Heedless to his pounding on the door, you refuse to open it. They don't know that they shouldn't interrupt your crying spells. Mr. Mostafavi will go and get the key to open your door. He doesn't know that you are only crying because you feel safe enough to do so behind the locked door. You aren't crying for someone to console you. You are crying because you simply feel like crying. Because moments of grief are simply anguish and pain. And for this reason, you slide the heavy table over and block the door so they won't be able to get in. Then you fall onto your bed and continue to weep. They don't know what to do. Your moaning is heartbreaking. It shakes everyone up and brings every listener and passerby to tears.

The first time you do this, Mr. Mollaei calls Parisa and she cries on the other end of the phone. Mr. Mollaei also cries himself. Parisa hangs up and calls back after twenty minutes. She explains how they are better off leaving you to yourself. The next time she speaks to you, she makes you promise not to cry anymore. She tells you a white lie that she will come to see you soon, but you don't believe her. "Soon" and "late" are alien concepts to you – just like earth and sky, happiness and sadness, or life and death. And whenever you miss yourself, me or Mom and Dad, your home and room, your music, or the picture of Angelina Jolie – Mrs. Smith that they will take away from you, you will take refuge in your bed, in your moaning and crying. Even right after a birthday party with music and dancing.

You open the shower door and step inside. You haven't turned on the water yet, when Parisa starts screaming and yelling again. "For God's sake! Pooya! Why are you doing this? Don't you know our guests are on their way here right now?"

Her cries are heartbreaking. she stands by the shower door, crying uncontrollably. she hits herself and curses everything and everyone – you, me, Mom and Dad. But mostly that good-for-nothing, Babak. This is the only thing I agree with Parisa about. Ever since he came into our home, things have gotten worse. Or maybe since he quit coming to our house – it doesn't make a lot of difference. How long did it take? Two years? Three years? Parisa changed completely. And when she came back, her fights with Mom started and your depression returned along with your reclusiveness, that I could understand. You had not yet recovered from your depression after Parisa's wedding. You had not yet bonded with Babak when you were forced to forget him forever. At first, you would listen to see what was going on, but you couldn't comprehend anything. And it was this not knowing and not understanding and this love on the edge of hate that confused you. Perhaps happiness and sadness don't mean anything to you, but you must know where you stand regarding love. You must know who to love and who not to love. The roots of your love take hold quickly, but pulling them out is like cutting off life itself. You must know whether to love or not.

And then Parisa and Mom's daily squabbles began about where Parisa went and what she did. What a fit she had when she found out that Parisa dropped out of college. You and I witnessed Dad laying a hand on Parisa for the first time. But Parisa very coolly followed her chosen path and continued taking the classes that Mom and Dad had forbidden her. Little by little, foreign words and changes in Parisa's appearance found their way into our home. Words like energy, chakra, chart, Reiki, and deliberate moon and mercury that she would explain on the telephone to her various new friends.

You turn on the water and take the shampoo. Mr. Safa had given you a shower the day before yesterday and you felt much better. You empty half the bottle of shampoo over the sparse hair on your head, and then start rinsing under the showerhead before having massaged it into suds. You wash your body superficially, turn off the water and step out without having rinsed well. Standing in front of the mirror, you plug in the electric shaver. Dad had taught you well how to shave without nicking your soft, fair skin. The coarse whiskers pepper the white sink. Heedless of the mess left behind, you put away the razor and emerge from the bathroom.

At the end of the hallway, Parisa quickly turns her head the other way, so as not to see your fat, white body and to let you know that she is upset with you. The doorbell rings. You leave your bedroom door open while you put on your clothes. From your bedroom at the end of the hallway, you look over the lady and gentlemen who enter through the front door. The lady is young and beautiful. She is wearing a red shawl. You still feel the warm water from the shower on your feet and back. You walk toward the front door, catching your foot on a box. You let out a loud yelp, and swear at Parisa in front of the lady customer in the red shawl, turning Parisa's face the same color.

The man wanders through the rooms and moves through the boxes from one side of the house to the other. He walks towards the stairway to go see the second floor. Parisa explains that your housekeeper, Mr. Safa and his wife live up there and will be moving in a couple of weeks and that it is really just a half level that you' have added on.

The man wants to tear down the house after a while and rebuild it. He draws out the negotiation for a month, using various faults about the house as an excuse to buy the house at a much discounted price. By that time, Parisa has left Iran and Aunt Fati, who is worn down by the man's constant haggling over the price, sells it to him cheaply by power of attorney on Parisa's behalf. Tuning out the man's calculating, home-buyer questions, you stand there with your attention fixed upon the quince-pink cheeks and red lips of the woman who obviously had a different destination today and was forced by the man into stopping at this house, no aspects of which spark her interest or curiosity.

Parisa does not go up to the second floor with the man. Mr. Safa's wife is at home and will show it to him. Parisa approaches the lady in the red shawl who is standing there, aloof, waiting for her man to come down quickly so that they can leave. The woman looks around disapprovingly at the house full of old, dusty houschold items and half-empty boxes. Then she looks Parisa up and down in the Bermuda shorts and old tee shirt she always wears at home, with her flattened hair clipped back behind her head, and the shawl thrown around her shoulders.

You walk toward her. She is startled and then hesitates, transferring her weight from leg to leg, like she is getting ready to run. You smile at her and your almond-shaped eyes get even tinier. She wants to return your smile but half-way into it she bites her lip and looks pleadingly at Parisa. Parisa comes forward and offers her a seat, and while looking daggers at you, she says, "Go to your room." But you don't take your eyes off the woman. Parisa tries to explain the events of the past year to the woman in the hopes that the demeaning look and surprise in her face will subside. She explains that Mom and Dad died in an accident a year ago and how she wants to sell the house and leave Iran. The woman nods her head at what Parisa tells her as she keeps an eye on you while you are inching closer to her. Parisa warns you and reluctantly tells the woman that she will have to commit you to an institution.

You abruptly say to the woman, "How bbeautiful yyou are! Wi wi will yyou ma ma marry mm mm me? I lo love you!"

The woman uncrosses her legs and sits straight in her chair, ready to get up and run out. When Parisa sees her uneasiness, she shouts at you, "Pooya! Don't start that again!"

You gesture to Parisa and turn to the woman and say, "Do do don't list listen to he her! Sh sh she's cra crazy!" And you keep getting closer and closer. Heedless to Parisa's warnings, you suddenly embrace the woman. Before the woman has the chance to get up and before Parisa is able to pull you away from her, you kiss her on the cheek but you immediately run back to your room at the sound of her terrified scream. Parisa is yelling behind you, as the woman uses tissue to wipe your slobber off of her face in disgust. You apologize and are at a loss as to what to say to her husband who has hurried down the stairs upon hearing his wife screaming and cursing, and is trying to calm her.

They start arguing and you listen from inside your room. Mrs. Smith gestures for you to go and see what is going on. You both walk out of your room together and just as Parisa is begging their pardon and the man and woman are ranting and raving, you walk into the living room. The man has made a fist and is standing there ready to pounce on you with an angry look on his face. But when he notices your short, fat body and almond-shaped eyes and rational look on your face, he gestures to his wife for them to get out of here. But you don't leave them alone.

As they are walking out of the living room through patio and courtyard, they pass the single persimmon tree as they walk out the door, you yell out and profess your love for the woman and ask her to marry you. Parisa, who can't control you, walks back inside the house with flushed forehead and blushing cheeks, heedless to the persimmon tree growing next to the wall, which had sweet, light-red fruit that lent color to the fruit basket every fall. The tree was Dad's favorite, which spread its green and orange umbrella not only over the courtyard, but over the outside of the courtyard wall, causing every passerby's mouth to water.

Yet this man whose name Parisa had not asked, and whom you would never see again, heedless to the fragrant shade of its leaves and green unripe fruit, pulls out the persimmon tree by its roots right at the beginning of harvest season this year and orders the house torn down to make way for a six-story apartment building.

Two

You don't know what time it is, Parisa. Your racing heart suddenly jolts you awake but your legs are still asleep. You force your eyelids open and turn the clock around on the bed stand to see what time it is. Then you gently close them again, comforted in knowing that you haven't overslept and can snuggle back into the warm, soft embrace of your bed for a while, stretch, and roll around until you wake up on your own. You roll the left side of your body away from the mattress until you no longer hear the reverberations of your heartbeat through your whole body and then you fall back asleep. You think it is good that you still have two hours to empty the contents of the bookshelves and the desk drawers before they come from Kahrizak to collect him. Little do you know they'll be here sooner and you will be forced to heap everything into a pile and deal with organizing and packing up the catastrophic mess later.

You suddenly remember the leftover chicken stew. You worry that Pooya has taken it out of the refrigerator and finished it all before leaving on the bus to the institute early that morning. And with all the work you have to get done today, you don't have time to cook and will have nothing to eat. Back before Mom died, she used to wake up every morning at 6:30 a.m. and see Pooya off on his school bus. After she read that story in the newspaper about the little Down 's syndrome boy who was abducted and raped, she began to worry more about Pooya and watched him more carefully. They found the twelve-year-old's body in a park after a week. God only knows how many times he was raped and by how many people. But you can't wake up early. You love the night and staying up late. Night time is when you are most active. You're not worried about Pooya anymore. He's a grown man and can take care of himself. If anyone tries to raise a hand to him, all he would have to do is push the person away with his heavy hand and that person would be laid out flat on the ground. One angry slap by Pooya's hand has the power to tear a person's ear drum. But you also know this, that when he is scared, he retreats into his shell like a turtle.

Your heart beats in the morning without any voluntary action on your part. It gets the blood flowing through each of the capillaries of your head and forehead, and whatever you do, your eyes won't stay closed. You get up and go into the kitchen quickly to check the refrigerator. Why the hurry? You know that in the end, you'll ultimately be faced with an empty dish. And that's exactly what happens.

Pooya woke up early that morning, got dressed, went into the kitchen and left nothing behind but a half liter of milk that he chugged straight from the milk bottle before leaving. You always rush when you want to find out the outcome of things. And that is how you will soon discover the dirty dishes from the chicken stew in the sink. What would be the difference between making sure about these things now versus a half an hour from now? Go ahead and sleep! I wish you'd never get up and I could come into your next dream, my sister. You have forsaken me just like Pooya did. You try not to dream about me. While all of these years all of this studying was to foretell events. I don't understand the desire to know bad events ahead of time. What profit was there in it for you to know about Mom's accident beforehand when you couldn't do anything to prevent it or my death? What were you able to do about the negative sign of an accident that you saw in my annual chart? What became of that? Well, now there is no need to hurry. Instead of foretelling bad events in our lives that seem to be fraught with nothing else, try to be a better medium. At least understand that my presence is because I'm worried about you and I understand the burden you carry on your shoulders is the heavy weight of your decisions and changes in your life.   You postpone your morning affirmations and mantras until later. You go towards the door, which is locked. You always lock it. Dad has asked you to never leave your bedroom door unlocked. At first, you were afraid of sleeping alone in a locked room. But there was no other choice. It wasn't worth the risk. If he had come after you at night, then what? Dad was sensitive to this point ever since the time Pooya tried to push you against the wall and harass you, and he realized what a predicament you were facing.

You were thirteen. Pooya was two years older than you. It was the end of spring, only a few days before the longest day of the year, the summer solstice. It was after eating Aashe Reshte. Pooya was restless. He didn't understand why his pants were suddenly tight at the zipper. You had just come out of the shower, and the fragrance of shampoo in your long, chestnut hair was diffusing throughout the house. Pooya was looking at your damp hair as you walked into the living room with eyes you remember as bloodshot, and then he attacked you in front of the horrified guests. The sound of the television news suddenly went quiet as Mom screamed and ran terrified from the kitchen into the living room and Dad leapt from his seat to reach you.

You didn't understand why Pooya, who was older than you on his birth certificate but whom you had always thought of as a little brother, wanted to hurt you. The Pooya you had played house and school with until just a few years before that – the Pooya who had always listened to you and performed the roles you made up for him in the games, even though he would get tired and abandon the game quickly, was pulling out the hair of your dolls and breaking the chalkboard you used to practice the ABC's on. He would beg you to teach him how to ride a bike. Mom had forbidden you two to go outside and play together. He would give you his fruit rolls for you to take him outside with you. He would beg incessantly, "Si..sis...sisty." You would take his cheese puffs and the bike, and ride two streets uphill together. You helped him with his short, fat legs onto the bike. You held the bike for him to get onto, right at the top of the hill. When you let go of the back of the bike, Pooya rode down the hill on the bike and then fell off onto the asphalt. His face was bloody, and his knees were skinned. You helped him up. He himself was quite shaken up, but still promised not to tell Mom about it. When you got home, you took him stealthily into the bathroom and cleaned up his wounds with a wet paper towel. You put an adhesive bandage on the scrape under his chin. The scar is still there.

Mom never found out what happened to Pooya that day. And you felt indebted to him for not telling on you. You always looked out for each other. Always. You waited in line for him for a swing at the park. When it was your turn, you would always call him over to get on after you. Each child could ride the swing ten times back and forth before it was time to hand over the swing to the next person in line. But if the kids in the park said even the slightest thing to Pooya or teased him, or laughed at his almond-shaped eyes or lisp, that little eight or nine-year-old Parisa would take them down with a beating so bad that their clothes would get all torn and dirty. Little by little you learned that cursing at them was more effective than fist fighting. Before leaving for the park, you would get your bad words ready in your mind; you would prepare the responses you would hurl at the children in the park if any of them dared to tease or make fun of Pooya. You thought that you were defending Pooya because he was your brother, because you loved him, because he was defenseless and you felt sorry for him. You thought that this was your duty. But you knew deep down inside, that you were really defending yourself. That you were defending against the common shame of having a retarded brother – a shame that you never felt nor were ever willing to withstand. You knew that if the kids succeeded in pointing fingers at Pooya, you would be next for being the sister of a mongol. You would never let that bad omen even come close to happening.

You did not sleep a wink all night. From the moment Dad pulled you out from underneath Pooya, until the next morning when he took Pooya to the doctor, he locked you both in your rooms. It was very difficult for you to process this incident that occurred right in front of Mom and Dad, Tooba, Papa Hamid and Aunt Fati. You felt like your reputation got smeared. Pooya broke your heart. It was as if he had betrayed all the love and purity of childhood. What was your solution? Turning your love for Pooya into eternal disgust for him, so that you would never harbor any expectations from him again, and never get hurt again. That whole night you thought about the past, the changes, and the terrible incident of that day, as you drowned yourself in self-hatred to no limit. From that night on, hatred didn't mean much anymore. It had lost its color. You were no longer able to love anybody nor hate them. And this hurt you greatly. You became entangled in a never ending cycle of loving and breaking off. You still wish to be able to love, even though you know that it's futile. That one experience you had with Babak proved it to you. At the beginning, you acted like you were in love. And then after that, no matter how much Babak would shout and curse during the usual, stupid arguments, you were never able to hate him.

You were caught up in your anger and hatred in the privacy of your own room until morning. You watched the hands of the clock turn until the dawn. Mom and Dad, who had not slept a wink all night either, came into your room before sunrise. They had to explain Pooya's sexuality to you, a girl who was still a child, and had not even experienced puberty yet. Mom discussed these things with you a few more times that day until nightfall, to teach you how to control your anger and hatred, and to forgive and to love again. She explained all the difficulties she had gone through since Pooya's birth and having nowhere to turn, and how much the uncontrollable consequences of it all hurt her. You tried to understand her, but you were still a child. So you swallowed your anger and for a few days you kept away from Pooya, who didn't understand why. Little by little, the hatred went away and so did the love. You locked the door on your feelings and threw away the key.

That week, Dad hired Mr. Safa, who was unmarried and recommended by Lady Azar from Shahmirzad. At the beginning, he would come twice a week to help with Pooya and chores around the house, and later when Dad built the flat on the top floor and he brought his wife to live there, he became part of the family. You turn the key in the lock, and walk into the kitchen in your top and pajama pants with your hair a mess. You know there is no one there, otherwise you would have covered yourself up a little better in front of Pooya. This way was safer for both of you. You gasp at the sight of the sink full of dirty dishes from last night's dinner. How great that you cannot hate Pooya. But in any case, you plan to scold him when he gets back. But until that time when he returns home, you become so busy preparing documents and papers that you completely forget that you haven't eaten lunch and Pooya is the reason for it.

You pour some oil into the frying pan and fry an egg for yourself. You have not yet sat down to eat when the doorbell rings. Before the people from Kahrizak come inside, you run and pull an A-line skirt over your pajamas, a duster over your top, and a shawl over your shoulders. Before they start taking the desk apart to transport it, you empty the drawers and then go over to the bookshelves. You clear all the books to one side. The room is full of books, papers, CD's and things that you have no idea what to do with: antique keys, a wristwatch, coins and broken pens and pencils. By the time they leave with the items (furniture) and you get back into the kitchen, the egg is no longer edible and the tea is cold.

You peel off the duster and take off the skirt and throw them onto the bed. You go back into the kitchen, empty the frying pan, light the fire under the tea, and suffice with bread and butter. Sitting among the boxes of books organizing papers and documents takes until evening. You get a big box ready for the books you intend to take to Shahmirzad. You're going to donate the old computer along with the books to the library in Shahmirzad. You page through the books one by one to make sure you haven't left anything important inside. You fill two big cartons with them. When you try to push the boxes over beside the wall, you realize you can't move them even an inch. So you get some smaller boxes and transfer the books into them. Now you're perspiring and exhausted. You feel weak. You go back into the kitchen for another bite of that bread and butter you ate at breakfast. Now for the papers and documents and things that were emptied out of the drawers from Dad's desk. You have been avoiding these drawers for a year. Only once were you forced to open them for the birth certificates. You opened them without really looking inside the drawers and facing Dad's personal belongings. It was right after his death, when you needed the documents for the hospital discharge and burial.

Now you don't know what to do with them. You take out a small box, but change your mind. You are afraid that if you spill water or something, you won't be able to protect Mom and Dad's last living documents. You bring Dad's old leather satchel that he kept behind the closet and is now lying next to the books all over the floor that you plan to keep. You place Mom and Dad's medical insurance booklet beside my birth certificate and social security card. You keep Pooya's handy to take over to the institution. Then you pause, pick up all three booklets and peel out the photographs. You kiss Mom's picture and look at mine. You miss her a lot more than me. Then you throw the rest of the booklets, pieces of paper and receipts into the trash. The birth certificates are enough. None of the other documents will ever be needed.

You open the satchel to put the birth certificates inside. You put your hand inside of the bag that seems empty, but you find a booklet with an old, leather cover inside the front pocket. It seems very old. You open it. The calligraphy script is written in blue ink that has smeared over time. You can't read it. It seems like a poem, a sonnet. You try to make out what it says and read it, but it's no use. you look at the first page of the booklet. It says, "Shahpour Khani-Porshokooh, June, 1941." Your guess is correct. This is granddad's poetry journal that Dad has carried around with him all these years. All these years he took it with him to class, meetings and parties! Losing his Dad must have been as hard for him as losing me, his son. After I was gone, he bonded with this journal more. Every night he would go to it and read its poems. Maybe he thought I was with his Dad and these poems would bring us all together, poems that were written from the heart for the heart. He always fret that he didn't have any tangible reminder of me. He turned my room inside out in the hopes of finding a sample of my handwriting, or anything that would remind him of me. But other than a package of cigarettes that I had hidden in my drawer, some heavy metal CD's and a few translations of western novels, there was nothing there for him to put in his satchel and carry around with him to feel close to me. And it doesn't matter to you. Even now you block me by letting the dust all over everything turn to mud, lest it remind you of me for one second. You have treated me this way from the very beginning, Parisa – without trust, consideration, attention or kindness. Maybe you were directing the anger, dread and caution you felt for Pooya toward me, and even toward all the men in your life. You turn the notebook in your hands, touch the binding and old, straw-colored paper carpeted with words, just like Shahpour did many years ago sitting underneath the mulberry tree of the Shahmirzad house. He rolled his pen in his fingers and touched the new paper in the journal as he opened his mind as a bridge for the words to flow out from his heart onto the paper. That was the day in June of 1941 when Shahpour bought the green journal from a store on his way home from the mosque. He had just seen Mahin for the first time. Sitting under the mulberry tree in the garden, he wrote his name and date on the first page and then set to turning all on the passion in his heart into poetry. From then on after that first spring day, he would wait outside the mosque every day after the noon and afternoon prayers to get a glimpse of Mahin leaving. With her inspiration, he would then sit underneath the old mulberry tree and compose another poem in his new journal. Shahpour's father was the Khan of Shahmirzad. His wine gatherings were notorious. But Mahin's father was the Mullah of the mosque.   Shahpour knew well that his father would never go for this match. Neither would he abide Shahpour's love for Mullah Hassan and his golden-haired daughter who was always covered by a chador. Her long, thick, golden hair that had never seen the sun was the morsel of every ladies circle, which intentionally or unintentionally reached the ears of all the young eligible men. The news of her beauty and golden braids eventually reached the ears of Nader, Shahpour's father. It had been at least a year since he had lost the power to stop his son from attending the mosque. Come rain or come shine, Shahpour never failed to offer his prayers at the mosque right at the appointed times. Shahpour's father preferred his only son to participate in his wine gatherings and drink with him and his guests. But Shahpour's reticence pained him. Shahpour never set foot in circles where drinking occurred.

The word was that Mullah Hassan had put a spell on Shahpour that made him follow him so devotedly. But this spell of Mullah Hassan was a different kind of spell; it was the kind of spell that could not be expressed. One year prior, Shahpour had gone to the town square to pick up a package that was to arrive for his father from Babol. The bus driver was handing him the package when his eyes caught sight of Mullah Hassan waiting for the bus. He was wearing a brown cloak and white turban and was standing there waiting for his suitcase to be unloaded from the bottom of the bus.

One of the passengers was making a scene and pretending to do magic. He told the second driver, "Say whatever you want! I will make something appear before your eyes." A boy said, "Two seeds, one good and one bad." The magician closed his eyes and chanted something. Two people made a step stool by intertwining their fingers and hoisted the second driver up so he could reach into the back corner of the overhead compartment, where he found two seeds - one good and one bad. He brought them down and showed them to everyone. The magician said, "My next magic trick will cost money. I will make whatever you wish appear, except money itself."

Mullah Hassan stepped forward. He stood behind the young man. He looked at his strong build and height, and his thick, black hair. His hands started shaking, and tears were streaming down his cheeks. He straightened his cloak and turban, took a deep breath and tried to contain the shaking in his voice. He said, "Seyed Hashem, is that you?"

The magician turned around and looked at Mullah Hassan. For a moment, his gaze paused upon Mullah Hassan's white hair and toothless mouth, as if he recognized him at once. He got ready to run and hide himself behind the bus. Mullah Hassan ran after him with all the people following behind. But the magician wasn't there. There was only a small boy standing there behind the bus. The people asked him where the young man went. The little boy had not seen anyone run this way. The young magician was never seen again in Shahmirzad.

Shahpour who had seen the magician's tricks and Mullah Hassan's encounter with him, escorted the Mullah to his new home in the hopes of finding out something more about the incident between the magician and the mullah. But the only thing he discovered was more about the new prayer leader of the mosque, who was supposed to move there with his whole family that next week.

Mullah Hassan spoke to Shahpour about God and the judgement day, and about this magic that the people were so entranced by. He told Shahpour all about how people fall into the temptation of magic and waste their lives and the lives of others. He recommended being a good, pure person, refraining from sin, praying at the appointed times, having a relationship with God through prayer and God's granting of prayers through prayer. He advised Shahpour about being a good human being all the way to his new home. This first session with Mullah Hassan fell like a brilliant white seal of God on his impressionable heart and left its mark for many years.

The distance Shahpour kept from Nader Khan's gatherings started long before his visits with Mullah Hassan. Even though Mullah Hassan was the only person who praised him for keeping this distance, his encouragement of Shahpour's restraint endorsed it.

Shahpour felt a sense of fear for these wine gatherings. It was an old fear tracing back to a night so long ago that the details had disappeared from his mind. He was only five-years-old. It was the end of June when days were hot but nights were cool; the desert nights made him shiver from the cold. The gathering that night broke the news of an important celebration. The hustle and bustle of the servants getting things ready and skewering the lamb meat had started that evening at sundown. What was strange was the unlike the rest of the guests who would be coming at the beginning of the night, the guest of honor would be coming at the end of the night. Father had sworn everyone who knew to secrecy regarding the identity of the guest of honor.

It was just past the middle of the cold of the night when after having a few glasses of Sekanjabin, his bladder couldn't take it anymore. He got up. There was no one in the room. You could hear the merrymaking and laughter from the living room, which was one of a row of rooms they had built side by side and was two doors down from his bedroom. The sky seemed to be getting light in the courtyard. He went into the courtyard. There were lanterns lit all around. There was a large number of armed men by the front gate and porch. As soon as the maid, Naeimeh saw Shahpour, she approached him to show him the way to the outhouse. Shahpour wasn't sure whether he was really awake or still asleep. He heard his father's chuckling and the merrymaking of the guests in the living room, which was a familiar sound to him.

Naeimeh was grumbling, "Don't say I didn't warn you! When this roof collapses on their heads it will be because of that sinful drink." He was still groggy walking aside Naeimeh when the front gate was kicked open. The soldiers rushed in and started firing. Naeimeh pushed Shahpour behind the outhouse before a bullet split open her chest and her blood-drenched body fell to the ground.

Ever since that night when by Reza Shah's direct order Nader promised in his private gathering to deliver over to the regime authorities Asghar the bandit, the most wicked bandit of Shahmirzad and Sangesar, he developed a phobia for going to the outhouse as well as for his father's festive gatherings. Nader scared all future maids for many years afterwards, that if they let out a word about Shahpour's night bedwetting or their having to wash the mattress and sheets daily, he would cut their throats from ear to ear.

Shahpour had seen Asghar the bandit once, but didn't remember it. He was not yet two-years-old when he was returning from Semnan to Shahmirzad with Nosrat his mother, his aunt and her husband. It was the end of the summer, and for the fall and winter ahead, they had gone shopping for bulk necessities at the Semnan bazaar: from fabric to yarn, boots, blankets, to rice, flour and spices. Nader had not been able to go with them and Nosrat insisted that they return from Semnan that night. Her toddler was exhausting her, and she wanted to get home as soon as possible. The bandits blocked their carriage near Sangesar. They forced out the passengers and the footman. Nosrat was shivering from fear and the cold, as she held Shahpour tight to her body. She felt things were not going to turn out well. Her fear was not of losing money, gold jewelry, or the goods they had just purchased. Her fear was to lose her child or her and her sister's dignity. As they were waiting by the carriage for the bandits to unload the bundles from the top of the carriages, she heard Asghar the bandit's name mentioned.

It took everything she had in her power. She borrowed from her love for Shahpour and her fear of losing him, and turned to one of the bandits pointing a gun at her. She said she was Nader Khan's wife, Asghar the bandit's friend. When they heard this, the bandits pulled back their bandanas. One came forward. It was Asghar the bandit himself. He apologized for not recognizing Nosrat and ordered all the bundles to be loaded back onto the carriage. He sent an armed escort with them back to Shahmirzad along with a warm greeting and apology to Nader Khan. And vanished into the darkness of the mountains with the rest of his men.

The next week Nader Khan threw a party for Asghar the bandit and his men. Asghar the bandit gave Nader Khan and Nosrat expensive gifts, from gold necklaces to Atlasi and Termeh - precious, handwoven fabrics. Nosrat wouldn't touch any of them; the thought of what poor woman's neck the necklace was torn from or from which defenseless traveler's bundle the gifts were stolen from in the middle of the night made her sick to her stomach.

Three years later when Nader Khan decided to cooperate with the Shah and turn in Asghar the bandit to the authorities, Nosrat was happy but nervous. She saw to every detail on the night they arrested him. But on that night after the unexpected murder of Naeimeh, and seeing the shock in the eyes of Asghar the bandit and his men by Nader Khan's unexpected betrayal, she knew that she would never see a safe night again. Fear of Asghar the bandit's revenge on her and Shahpour's nightly bed-wetting shook Nosrat and Nader's peace from that night on.

Shahmirzad wasn't a big town. Talk got around. As if Shahpour's notoriety for timidness and bed-wetting was not enough, that constantly praying at the mosque, falling in love with Mullah's daughter and poetry writing was added to it. Nader consulted every physician for a cure of his bed-wetting. They tried every herb and medicine to no avail. No matter how many blankets they wrapped around his waist to keep him warm at night was not helping. Nader didn't believe in spells. Nosrat had heard from the women in the town that it would help if Shahpour took a wife. Nosrat wanted to have him marry her brother's daughter, but her fear that marrying might not help in the end and embarrass her even more in front of friends, family and neighbors, she didn't dare act on it.

When she heard all about her son's love affair she told one of the household maid watch for when Mahin and her mother next go to the public bath and let her know. When she saw Mahin in the public bath washing her long, blond hair and tossing it over her fair, porcelain shoulders, she understood her son's infatuation, and without admitting to Mahin's overwhelming beauty, she couldn't blame Shahpour for wanting this girl. Nosrat kept whispering in Nader's ear that this was the best way – that they should let him marry Mullah's daughter for now, and whenever Shahpour's problem was resolved, they would make her lose favor in his eyes and find a suitable wife for him. Nader knew that there was nothing else he could do. He couldn't stand up to Nosrat's wishes and their good-for-nothing only son. He ordered Nosrat and the maids to spread the rumor of Mahin's beauty and dreamy, blond locks so far that people would easily justify the match of a girl with legendary beauty who could only be suitable for the most eligible young man of the town, Nader Khan's son.

Shahpour's poetry writing and bed-wetting ended after the engagement party. What need was there for writing poetry? The poem itself was now a figure before his eyes. It wasn't Mahin's blond hair and hazel eyes that found their place in the hearts of Nader and Nosrat, but it was her gentle kindness that made everyone fall in love with her.

The wedding party was a sumptuous event in Shahmirzad. Mullah Hassan had requested them not to hold the kind of party that he could not attend. So they gathered up and took away all the wine in respect of Mullah Hassan presence. But Nader Khan started having a party of his own right after the guests left and the bride and groom had retired to their conjugal room. He drank until morning and made several of the maids come into his room to sing and dance for him. He partied like never before.

When Mahin stepped out of her bedroom to freshen up on the first morning of her married life, she came face to face with Nader's dead body. It wasn't clear at what early morning hour he had emerged dead drunk from his room, caught his foot on the edge of the fountain, and fell to the ground, shattering his temple and causing Mahin to carry that inauspicious label of bad luck on her shoulders from that day forward. Little by little, she started applying brown henna to her golden hair, which had become an ominous symbol. The longer the time passed without conceiving a child, the browner and shorter her hair became. But it was no use. What mattered was Shahpour, who had become disenchanted with Mahin, the mosque and Mullah Hassan on that first morning when his married life became intertwined with mourning and loss. He himself never thought that his father's death would affect him so deeply. He never imagined that his father had such a place in his heart. He blamed the loss of his father on his own selfishness, and saw Mahin as the root of it all. As the wine glasses were passed around at Nader's funeral, he picked his father's legacy and made it his own. He couldn't face Mullah Hassan anymore.

With the first year anniversary of Nader's death and still no news of a child, Tayebeh entered their lives.

She was Shahpour's luckless cousin, whose wealthy, influential father had recently started up a grocery goods warehouse and had increased his investment manifold by the grace and kindness of the Shah. Three years passed since her fiancée had died from snakebite, and due to her sulky demeanor and stormy disposition, she still had no offers of marriage. Tayebeh was the same age as Mahin, but unlike Mahin, she was olive-skinned, with black, curly hair and a hawkish nose. She was tall and exuded a sense of authority amongst the maids. Mahin, who had become depressed, would take leave and go to her father's home on nights when she knew there would be no affection forthcoming from Shahpour. She would spend those nights beside her grieving mother, who was still dealing with the death of her sons, and with her dear father.

When there was still no sign of a child a year later, Tayebeh's mother and father brought her home from Shahpour's house by force, because they blamed her childlessness on Shahpour's inability to produce a child. They had the right. A man who cannot produce a child with two wives is likely the one at fault. They therefore demanded and collected her full dowry, which was one-third of the land.

Tayebeh never married again.

But Nosrat didn't just sit there. This time she was smart in choosing a bride who would not require a hefty dowry; a girl who would marry a man whose only inheritance was his father's love for drink – a girl who would be willing to become a third wife. And that was how this young, pubescent orphan whose grandfather had sent from the village of Sefioun to work there as a maid was married off to her son. Azar was no more than thirteen years old. She was fair with a freckled face and a thin nose. She was tall and thin with unusually rosy lips. She was unpretentious, unexperienced and unmotivated. At the beginning, she worked as a maid and kept Shahpour's bed warm at night. Mahin had moved into the next bedroom months ago, and every night she prayed that God smile upon them and let unlucky Azar conceive a child so that perhaps Shahpour and Nosrat's disposition would change and life would stop being the hellish situation she was contending with.

But two years passed and Azar, a teenager who was just beginning to fill out and was becoming a beautiful young woman, was finding refuge and peace in Mahin's room from Shahpour's drunken abuse of her. This made Mahin happy, for she did not have a brother or sister, and her husband turned out cold and unaffectionate, and she had no child to love. A bond gradually formed between Mahin and Azar that caused both of them to become more dependent on each other than ever before; it was a genuinely sisterly friendship. They spent all day together, slept next to each other and woke up together. They went out together and shared all their secrets with each other.

Until gradually the rumor of the mulberry tree spell disturbed the relative quietness that existed at home before Shahpour's overdrinking. Shahpour would get so drunk that he would sit there sobbing, without any thought as to the whereabouts of his wives or what they were doing; he totally ignored them. People said that Shahpour's mother was jealous of Mahin's beauty at first, and in order to destroy the love of her only child for her, she buried a talisman in the garden and later forgot where in the garden she had buried it, and that her actions caused Nader's death and Shahpour's inability to produce a child. Other's thought it was Asghar Yaghi's curse. Some people said that right before Asghar Yaghi's execution, he had met with one of Nader's maids in the jail and had given her a large sum of money to bury a talisman underneath the mulberry tree so that he could take vengeance on Nader.

What all the rumors indicated was the existence of a talisman of hate which was probably buried in the garden under the mulberry tree, aimed like an arrow at all the household members and marking the fate of Shahpour's childlessness. By Shahpour's orders to put all rumors to rest, the whole garden was dug up and the dirt overturned; but nothing was found.

The news of Mullah Hassan's death reached Shahpour's home on the evening of the day they dug up the garden. The whole town was in mourning. For Mahin, losing her father was unbearable. Every night she cried silent tears until morning; and while she kept herself from moaning and wailing out loud, Shahpour could still hear the sound of her soft crying on the other side of the wall of the adjacent room. Hearing the heart wrenching crying until morning cleared the sleep from his eyes. He listened to the sound of her wailing all night and remembered the things Mullah Hassan had talked about. It made the wine on his breath taste like poison.

One night when Shahpour had had enough of Mahin's wailing, and no amount of cotton stuffed into his ears was doing any good, and no amount of wine was helping him fall asleep, he went to his poetry journal where he used to write down his overflowing feelings. He missed Mahin and himself, and he missed the simplicity and sweetness of those days. He felt that he had to repent. He knew well that it was his drinking that robbed him of Mahin and the happiness of those days. And this is why he resolved to go on pilgrimage. On the fortieth day after Mullah Hassan's death, he took Mahin's hand and went to Mashad.

Three months later, Mahin returned to Shahmirzad carrying his child, and in December of 1951 our father, Ali was born at a house in Shahmirzad that became the only legacy of a once-illustrious Khan, before the land reform act and mandatory turnover of farmlands, walnut and apricot orchards to farmers.

That spring, the old mulberry tree no longer yielded fruit since they had dug up the dirt beneath it. In the middle of the fall, they pulled out the dried up tree by its roots and dumped the bulky trunk into the river.

Three

You press the intercom button to open the door and put the kettle on before Fati comes up. Then you go check on Pooya to see how he is doing. You hear his music playing, but the volume is not very high, which means his imaginary guests haven't arrived yet. You don't knock. It's better to just let him be and have his party as long as Fati is here. You tiptoe quietly back into the kitchen. These actions of yours are automatic. It's obvious by the tone of the music that Pooya hasn't heard your footsteps. And even if he had heard you, he wouldn't have come out of his room unless you begged him. But just the fact that his music isn't deafening the whole house is a little suspicious. And you feel this.

She smells like mother, and you can't make yourself let go of her. A tear rolls down your cheek. Aunt Fati thinks you're already homesick, and you act like she is right, rather than letting on that you are really just missing mother.

When you have your tea, you start boxing up the items in the kitchen. You go to the stairs of the second floor and call Mr. Safa's wife to come and have the dishes you and Aunt Fati don't want to keep. You put the rest of the dishes and pots and pans into a box to take to Shahmirzad.

Pooya's stereo volume is moderately high. You want to check on him and see what he is doing, but it isn't worth the risk. He might suddenly become aware of Aunt Fati's presence and go to pieces. Leave him to his own peace. Don't worry. It's true that he hears you and what is going on in the house, but he is pouring out his heart to his imaginary guests. He is in the middle of an important talk with father. He wants to buy a car. He is asking father whether a 206 is a good car to buy, should he get black or red, and which is more masculine. He hasn't yet decided to make a scene.

Mr. Safa's wife comes limping down the stairs. She showed no interest in looking through the second-hand dishes, some of which were thirty or forty years old.

One by one, you wrap up the old-fashioned Royal Albert New Country Roses dishes with the blaring rose design in newspaper and place them inside the boxes. Aunt Fati wraps up the Country Roses teacups. You wonder when these dishes were made, when were they bought? Wasn't there a nicer pattern to buy back then? You have no point of reference except for Pooya's birthday. One year prior? Two? Three years? You don't know. You don't know what year mother and father married. You never asked. It was never important to you. Nothing was ever important to you except your own goals. And now you are ashamed of asking Aunt Fati. How could she ever understand such a deep rift between a mother and a daughter.

Fati asks what you plan on doing with the set of china dishes? You shrug. When you see her surprise, you ask her to keep them for you. Whatever the case, they are a keepsake from mother's trousseau, which she never wanted to use except for special occasions. In the early days, we used to eat out of melamine dishes. Now eat out of inexpensive Iranian Arcopal dishes. You know you'll never lay eyes upon these dishes again, but from now on you'll only see them in your dreams during the long, cold nights in Montreal. In the corner of your dream, you'll see a Duchess Rose teacup or a plate. People in your dreams always eat heavy yogurt soup in New Country Roses bowls. People who never ate anything before in your dreams. You have seen yourself many times holding a New Country Roses fruit plate in your hands while you look for something to put in it. Sister dear, it will take many years for you to turn Pooya into a memory, and for our mother Zari's absence to become normal for you, and for the New Country Roses dishes to fade from your dreams. That is when I will be your guest at night. The nightmares needed some time to soak into your subconscious and spread their roots down to penetrate the innermost layers of your dreams. That is when you will see me in your dreams: in a dream where I am a child following you down the porch stairs in Shahmirzad into the garden. Your skirt was blowing in the wind, and the wind made waves your sable hair. I call out to you. "Parisa! Parisa!" It is my voice as a child. I beg you to turn around and look at me. You turn around and look at me. At first it looks like a New Country Roses flower is stuck on me below my stomach. You come closer. The flower gets bigger and bigger, and the blood-like redness takes over my whole body, and blinds you. You hear Pooya screaming and wake up. Lucky for the psychologists and therapists who make good money interpreting your dreams. That is when Reiki no longer does any good, neither do mantras, yoga, affirmations or even Xanax or Clonazepam. It is when you have lost hope in everything, and you only want to talk to someone about your nightmares, about me, about Pooya, about our mother Zari, and about all the memories and feelings you have buried in the layers of your consciousness.

Mr. Safa's wife handles the dishes as if they are dirty. She picks up the bowls and pots by the edge with her fingers and examines them. This offends you. As if anything but food was served in these dishes for her to look them up and down in disgust. She acts as if she is doing you a favor by taking them off your hands for free. She picks up a small omelet skillet that you used and she smells it. You've had enough, but you try to control yourself. You grab the skillet from her and tell her in a respectful tone of voice that you've changed your mind and have decided to keep everything on the chance that you might end up coming back sooner and need them after all. Mr. Safa's wife picks up her calico skirt with that same indifference and goes back upstairs, neither happy nor sad.

You don't allow Aunt Fati to talk behind her back. You say it brings bad Karma. Aunt Fati asks, "You mean that gossiping is a sin?" You have no answer for all of these words have the same meaning in your mind: sin, good deeds, karma, and the consequence of one's actions all mean the same thing to you. You know that bad deeds carry bad energy which affects you in this lifetime and good deeds carry good energy. Aunt Fati went on with her usual advising and grumbling like Maman Zari who was always nagging and criticizing. She would say that there was no future in fortune-telling and the same for going to Canada, let alone living your life this way there. You don't get into it with her and argue that fortune-telling is not your profession. Astrology is a science. You have said this for years, but nobody would ever listen. Whenever the discussion reached this point, you would always have to change the subject. Arguing and explaining was no use. If they wanted to accept it, they would have accepted it by now. Your Guru had forbidden you to defend your science needlessly.

Pooya's stereo stopped. You hear the door to his room open. His heavy steps reverberate down the hallway to the kitchen. You close the kitchen door so that he might pass by and head for the living room instead. How nice that the old fashioned kitchens aren't open. They have walls and doors so that neither the smell of fried onions and dirty dishes will permeate through the house, nor will the clutter and mess make the disarray in the living room seem much greater. You could never stand open-concept kitchens.

Babak's rental apartment had a small kitchen the same width as the living room. The dark, tight space in the kitchen with those small cabinets that you were never able to fit the dishes in, drove you crazy. Babak was always frustrated that you couldn't keep your kitchen tidy, and that your burned cooking oil stunk up the whole house. You would get even more frustrated that Babak would never take his eyes off the TV screen, get up off the couch and come help out in the kitchen and make you something to eat for once. Babak would get angry because he thought of this as your duty and he was exhausted from study and work, that as he said, he did for your sake. You would get even angrier because you were in class all day and believed you had every right to attend to your own personal and social life. Babak would turn red and start yelling, "What is the meaning of a woman out roaming around at this time of night, ignoring her husband and duties at home? A woman's duties are clear: homemaking and taking care of her husband and children!" You would laugh and Babak would explode and throw and break all the dishes, and people could hear his unanswered howling several blocks away. You would escape his kicks and punches by running to your car.

Aunt Fati won't let well enough alone. It's like she's trying to bring you to your senses all in one day. But you won't give in either. To change the subject, you take two notebooks that you have found recently down off of the top of the refrigerator and show them to her. The first one is your paternal grandfather, Shahpour's poetry notebook. Aunt Fati puts it down with disinterest and moves on to the next one, a 200-page black, leather bound notebook. Fati opens it and asks with surprise, "What is this blank notebook?" You tell her that it is the one she has been looking for and has asked you to let her know if you find it so that she can read it – Maman Zari's diary where she was going to write life story. You show her the first page; a paragraph and a family tree scribbled there. But you still haven't uncovered the good part of it. You tease her with some sheets of paper you pull out from inside the book. These are a few old letters, some newspaper clippings of literary writings and poems from before the revolution, Reza Poursalari's newspaper obituary on paper that is now worn and yellowed from time. Aunt Fati is tantalized by all this. She takes them from your hands.

Suddenly Pooya bursts through the kitchen door. His eyes fall upon Aunt Fati and starts yelling, "Get...lo...lost!" You grab his arms in mid-air that he has raised to hit her as she runs around the kitchen table. He yells, "Let me go!" and he swears at you at the top of his voice. "You son of a...l...l...let m...me ...go! I'mm...gon..na...k...kill...her!" You try to calm him down. When he's angry, he doesn't understand anything. Aunt Fati runs toward the kitchen door and out to the patio. As you try to bar Pooya with all your strength at the kitchen door, he pulls out some china dishes that you have just wrapped up and packed in the boxes by the door and throws them at Aunt Fati. You slap him across the ear and let him go so that you can go and pick up mother's country rose dishes off the floor as if to save them before they die. But you can't. Three plates and a cup have shattered into pieces all over the living room. You yell at Pooya that you are fed up with his actions. Of course, you know well that this is futile. You soften your tone and tell him to be careful not to step on the broken china pieces. He doesn't listen. He just walks right through it, leaving a trail of blood on the wood floor back to his room. You bring the broom and dust pan and sweep up the pieces. For the first time, your eyes fall upon the words "made in England" on the back of one of the broken dishes. You make some ice water and walk out to the patio. You don't know how to apologize for what happened. But Fati is sitting there ensconced in reading a hand-written letter from Uncle Reza, who years ago Mostafa, the father of our grandmother, by her taste bought this very country rose china service for Tooba's trousseau. Tooba never used the set and saved it for her daughter Zari's wedding.

The English china set was a part of Tooba's expensive trousseau that Mostafa had procured in England and brought back with him one trip prior to his last trip to Europe. He was still at the peak of his wealth and best circumstances then, and never imagined that he would lose everything in a few months and end his life right there in his room at the Grand Hotel in London near Trafalgar Square with a shotgun he had purchased on a prior trip to London and that he kept in his bank safe deposit box.

He had taken his son, Reza on those two last trips. Both trips were taken less than six months apart. Mostafa was a businessman. At first, he worked mostly with Russia, exporting dry foodstuffs, sesame seed, cotton, jute, wool and other things, and importing from there fragile dishes, samovars, sugar and fabrics. His largest transactions were in exporting wool to Turkey and cotton to Europe. Mostafa Poursalari was summoned on the second to his last trip by invitation through the British embassy for suspending business contracts. As soon as he reached London, he realized that because the oil industry in Iran had been nationalized by Dr. Mossadegh, in response, the British ordered ships not to take delivery of any more cotton from Iran and pursued this policy in general with regard to all business transactions with Iran. No amount of consultation did him any good. He had to return for Tooba's wedding. All the money he had, he spent on his daughter's wedding gown fabrics, personal toiletries and dishes for his daughter and shoes and suits for his son. When he returned, he had a great amount of cotton on his hands that was left unsold and didn't know how to sell it. He sold some of it at a three-million-toman loss in the Iranian bazaar. And he used some of it to pay his creditors. At the end of June when Reza's illness began, the creditors formally demanded payment of their promissory notes, so that high profit transactions with Spain would save him from ending up in debtor's jail. In Spain, they contacted Shahi Bank for a referral of a trustworthy businessman for transactions in pharmaceutical grade opium. Mr. Moluki knew of Mostafa and was aware of his situation and so he referred him.

This wasn't the first time that Britain had put Mostafa in jeopardy of bankruptcy. Ten years before that when everybody was talking about famine and the entry of Triple Entente Troops into Tehran and Reza Shah's fleeing the country, Mostafa was left with six-hundred tons of wool on his hands. The domestic changes occurring in Iran had brought about a situation where the demand of wool had suddenly disappeared in the market. After much fruitless discussion with the government, the parliament and finance ministry, Mostafa sent epistles to the British, Russian and Turkish embassies inviting their business cooperation. The embassies didn't answer him, but a Turkish businessman after a couple of months of correspondence through letters and telegraph, showed interest in buying the wool at four times the going price, even though it wasn't clear practically how this could be achieved. In the final moments of hope of receiving the intended deposit, Mostafa received a letter from the British embassy inviting him there. When Mostafa Poursalari went to the embassy, he saw that the British had transcripts of all correspondence between him and the Turkish businessman, and it was quickly communicated to him that the transaction of wool with Turkey must be cancelled because they believed the wool was intended to be sold to Germany. They threatened that if he did not do so, his name would be blacklisted.

In the months following, Mostafa failed in achieving his aim no matter where he turned. One day at the Mohammad Beik Public Bath, the masseuse told him that it was his final days and that he was packed and wanted to say goodbye to Mostafa. Mostafa played it off as a joke and told Mohammad Beik, "Well, if you're really leaving, then say hello to my father and tell him to pray for my troubles to end." Mohammad Beik said cheerfully that he would indeed do so. Then he sloughed Mostafa's back vigorously and brought hot water for him. That memory of his last bath at the Mohammad Beik Public Bath always stayed with him. He had been renewed, and not just his body, but it was as if his spirit and life had been washed clean too. Two days later Esfandiari, Mostafa's father's old friend, contacted him from the finance ministry and said, "Your father came to me in a dream last night. He wanted me to help solve your problem." That night, Mohammad Beik had died. Mr. Esfandiari, using his contacts, was able to buy 600 tons of cotton from Mostafa at the government rate, the profit of which was enough to cover the loss of not selling the wool.

With all the ups and downs, highs and lows in business and finance, the fame of Mostafa Poursalari and his brother, Morteza who was his partner in business, on the surface seemed to burn all of those who were jealous of them, but in truth, because of the many troubles they had to contend with on a daily basis, it burned them up from within. The only thing that made Mostafa happy in life was his six children: his five daughters and surprise son, Reza. His youngest daughter, Tooba, had just become engaged to Hamid, his brother's son when Reza's headaches started.

At the beginning, Reza would say that his head itched intensely. He would scratch his forehead and the back of his head. But he kept getting more and more listless and weaker, always tired and never in the mood. He looked yellow and gaunt. For months he went from physician to physician to find out what was wrong with him. Finally, a doctor who had just come back from abroad by the name of Dr. Mansouri who worked at Shafa Hospital in Tehran, whom they said treated the incurable, gave the order for various laboratory tests. The prognosis did not look good. When Mostafa and Reza returned from receiving Dr. Mansouri's final diagnosis, all his daughters, their husbands and children gathered around Mostafa at his house to see what was wrong with their fourteen-year-old brother. Tooba and her fiancée Hamid were there too. Mostafa hid the flames that were burning inside of him and tried to behave normally so they wouldn't see the fire of fear and terror in his eyes. With their mouths open in awe and their eyes fixed upon father's lips and Reza's skinny, frail body as he slipped off his shoes, they all waited for the prognosis. Mostafa said that Dr. Mansouri's diagnosis was leukemia. Reza's mother, Matineh's joy and happiness rang out through the speechless silence of those gathered there as she held him in her arms and kissed him, saying "Thank God it isn't tuberculosis!"

Heedless of Dr. Mansouri who advised that there was no cure for leukemia abroad, Mostafa took Reza to London using the remaining funds from the opium sales. In their father's and Reza's absence, the girls stayed by their mother's side. Their most recent pastime was reading the letters that Reza sent them every day from the Royal Hospital of London; letters that would reach them in only a few short days. Tooba and Tahereh were literate. Whenever Tooba's morning sickness subsided, she would read the letters to them, otherwise the task would pass to Tahereh, who of course, wasn't a good a reader as Tooba was.

Reza wrote stories about the interesting things he saw in the hospital. These stories would keep his sisters and their offspring busy all day as well as his mother, who carried the great weight of worry for her daughters as she grappled with the daily responsibilities of cooking, cleaning and serving guests. He wrote about the nurses who wore short, white skirts; Reza in his mischief had several times succeeded in catching a glimpse under them! He also wrote about the atmosphere in the hospital and about the building itself, which was eight stories, with 400 rooms and seven elevators. His descriptions about what an elevator was and how it worked amazed everyone. A small room that moved between the stories, and would stop at the corresponding floor to the number displayed above the door that would light up. Once out of mischief, he rang the emergency bell and ran back to his bed. The nurse, thinking that one of the patients was dire need of help, searched all over but never found the patient. Reza did this again, but this time the nurse came immediately and scolded him because she realized he was playing tricks on her, and this caused a real fight to break out between them.

Reza wrote to them about the tall pine tree growing outside his room at the hospital. The tree grew right next to the building and its branches touched his room's window glass on the third floor. Reza had grown fond of listening to the sounds, watching the passersby and the flight of the sparrows from their nests in the pine tree. Once he decided to open the window and put out some bread crumbs for the sparrows. The tree branch lurched into the room, and he wasn't able to get the branch out of the room and close the window no matter how he tried. The nurse wasn't able to get the branch out either, and the freezing cold of London that came into the room through the window along with the pine needles wasn't good for Reza at all. The nurse called her supervisor in to cut the branch and close the window.

Reza had written in his letter to his mother and sisters that he heard the tree cry every night after they cut the tree branch. In the morning, he no longer heard the singing of the happy sparrows at sunrise. In his last letter, he had written that the sparrows in the pine tree outside his window weren't talking to him anymore, nor was the tree. He wrote that the hospital atmosphere was depressing for him and that he wanted to come home as soon as possible. There was no news from Reza for two weeks until finally a telegram came for Matineh that informed her of the death of her son. Mostafa locked himself inside his hotel room. He was neither able to cry nor talk. He just stayed in his room alone grieving for his only son morning. In the afternoon on the day after Reza's death, the concierge couldn't get anyone to open the door no matter how many times he knocked. He pushed two four-folded documents under the door. The first was a telegram informing him of the fire and sinking of the ship carrying the cargo load of cotton that Mostafa and his brother were shipping to France. After the high-profit opium contract and taking out a large loan from Melli Bank, Mostafa invested everything he had to make up for his prior failed investment after the breach of contract. The second telegram was from the hospital requesting him to release Reza's corpse from the cold storage in the hospital. Two minutes later, the sound of Mostafa firing the bullet into his mouth rang out, waking the travelers from their afternoon naps with a start.

The telegram about Mostafa's suicide reached Matineh's hands only hours after she received the news of Reza's death. After that, it took some time for Morteza to go to England and return to Tehran with the bodies of his brother and nephew. The grieving went on for forty days. Matineh cried so incessantly that people wondered where all these tears came from. Her sister in law, Malakeh was telling people that she hid a vile of water under her handkerchief and poured the fake tears on her cheeks when no one was looking. Masoumeh, her oldest daughter, in order to bring an end to such talk, collected her mother's tears in a crystal vase over a one-day period. When she emptied the vase in front of the women of the family as they looked on in shock, there was the equivalent of four glasses of liquid. Matineh barely ever needed to go to the bathroom for those forty days. She couldn't sleep and she wouldn't eat. All the liquid she drank was excreted through her tears. She wouldn't touch food. Only once in a while she might allow them to put a small taste of hard sugar or bread into her mouth. She just cried all the time. She wasn't sleeping no fully awake. Little by little, her pupils turned white. Her eyelids wouldn't close. She would pace the house in the middle of the night, weeping as she walked to and fro. Sometimes she would catch her foot on something and fall down. Her daughters would take turns staying up all night with Matineh and watching after her. On the weekends, her sisters would come to help. In the end, the things she was saying weren't making any sense. They said she was talking to ghosts and genies. She was delirious and speaking and sometime yelling at figments of her imagination. More rational people explained that accepting the loss of her husband and only son all at once was impossible for her and made her lose her mind.

The day that our mother Zari was born, Tooba with her big stomach, had walked all night beside Matineh, watching out for her mother not to trip and fall. It was close to the morning call to prayer when Tooba's water broke. Matineh was wandering through the kitchen and the rest of the rooms in the house that they had cleared out. Tooba yelled for help, but no one heard her. Tooba limped out to the yard and passed out there. Matineh, with her blind eyes, walked into the doorframe and fell to the ground.

Hamid who after his morning prayers had gone to buy fresh bread to bring over to Matineh's house for breakfast, after which he would take his wife home, saw the gate open and his wife lying on the ground. He brought Tooba back into the house and went after her sisters and the midwife. He picked up Matineh, who was passed out on the kitchen floor, put her into bed and went to get a doctor. When Tooba came to, she saw the midwife in front of her and felt like her legs were being ripped from her body at the hips. She wanted to get relief from the exhausting pain. The pain travelled up through her throat and turned into a scream.

Hearing Tooba's scream and the cries of the newborn, Matineh came to for a moment. She asked the young doctor attending her what was going on. The young man congratulated Matineh on her grandchild. She asked, "How long have I been like this? Why can't I see anything?" The doctor answered, "About two months. You've cried so much, you've gone blind." Matineh said she knew why, and it wasn't because of grief. She said that the loss of her son and husband still squeezed her heart. The young doctor wasn't sure whether Matineh was really coherent, or whether these things were part of her hallucinations. Then Matineh took his hand and said firmly, "Give me something to end this. End my life and this tragedy. This will be better for my daughters."

The young man pulled back his hand in horror, and tried to console Matineh. But she wasn't having any of it. She begged and she pleaded. She prayed and cursed him until she passed out. When she came to, still groggy, she wanted to get up and start wandering the house like before. Everything was so chaotic. People were coming and going inside the house, taking basins, bringing hot water, making food; every person was busy doing some task. The young doctor looked at Matineh's two broken legs, her back that was likely paralyzed and her blind, white eyes, and he felt a sense of honor for all the tolerance her family members had shown her. He could hear the baby crying as the women rushed throughout the house. The young doctor took out a vile from his leather bag. He dropped a drop of cyanide under Matineh's tongue and quietly left there never to return.

Four

You bend over to see how badly ripped your pant leg is. Your thin, light brown hair sticks to the leather of the seat and the static electricity in the leather causes it to stand on end. You don't see it yourself. Mr. Habibi watches you from behind in the mirror and says it is dangerous. It would be better for you to lean against the back of the chair. You let his words go in one ear and out the other.

You keep your wide back bent over and turn your head toward the window and point to your pant leg and ask mother, "Wi…wi..will sh…she get ma…mad at me?" You mean Parisa. You don't know what she will do about your torn pant leg. If it were mother, you would be certain she would yell at you, but then kiss you almost immediately and make up. But you cannot ever predict what Parisa will do. Sometimes she screams and yells over the tiniest little thing and other times, she won't get angry no matter how hard you try to annoy her. You look in another direction toward Mrs. Smith wearing her short red skirt with her legs crossed showing off her long, fair-skinned legs to get advice. She nods her head in agreement. It's the best thing to do. Parisa must not find out that you ripped your pant leg. You straighten your back and sit down. You take Mrs. Smith's hands in your hands. Her nails are long and polished. You bring her hand up to your cracked, chapped lips and kiss it. Mrs. Smith smiles in gratitude.

You are happy to be such a handsome gentleman, sitting calmly next to your lovely sweetheart until the driver from the school driving an Arrow, which you envision as a magnificent limousine delivering you to a luxurious castle. You straighten the collar of your t-shirt, still dirty from the fight today. It must be smooth and straight underneath your tie. When you get home, you don't get out of the car. You wait for Mr. Habibi to open the door for you. At first he wouldn't do it and would fuss and balk, "Let yourself out of the car!" But little by little he accepted the fact that you would sit there until the driver would open the door for you, important person that you are, to step out onto the red carpet just like in the movies and walk into your castle with your beautiful lady.

You get out. You take out your key and walk quietly into the house. Mrs. Smith whispers that Parisa should not know about this and you nod and say you know. Parisa is in the kitchen on the phone. She doesn't see you from there. You walk into your bedroom and lock the door behind you. Parisa has taken away the key to your room many times, but you tear the house apart to find it wherever it is. The last time your tore up Parisa's lingerie drawer and found the key, she stopped caring about hiding it from you.

You take off your pants and start in on them with a pair of scissors. You haphazardly cut them to pieces and cut your leg in the process. Your t-shirt is dusty and dirty, and has a pungent smell of sweat. You sniff your underarm and notice that the smell is not much different than your t-shirt. You take a can of deodorant spray off the dresser and spray so much under your arms that you leave a residue of white talc on your skin. You pick up the pieces of pants and your dirty clothes and walk naked to the shower. You aren't in the mood to shower, though. You throw your dirty clothes in the hamper, and the pieces of your pants into the trash can in the shower. Then you look through the residue on the dirty mirror of the bathroom cabinet that Parisa hasn't cleaned since mother died. You run your hand over the old scar under your lip. You don't know what difference it makes. You think you are neither ugly nor handsome. You don't perceive your looks correctly. You never put yourself to the test. Perhaps you know subconsciously it would have terrible consequences. Your tiny, almond-shaped eyes and your yellow teeth make it worse. They have never succeeded in getting you to brush your teeth, and you still will not do it.

It doesn't matter. Mrs. Smith loves you just the way you are. From looking at your image in the mirror, you don't come to any conclusion, but you only find comfort that there is no evidence of today's fight on your face. You take out a green, plastic bottle of betadine from the cabinet and empty it on the scratches on your calf. The whole shower floor turns blood red from the betadine, and heedless of the fact that your ankle is still dripping, you step out and walk back to your room.

You put on a comfortable pair of shorts and a t-shirt and go into the kitchen to see if you can find something to eat. Standing by the kitchen door, Parisa asks, "Where is your 'hello'?" You yell, "G…get…outta…my….w…way!   I   w..want… some..thing…to eat!" Parisa has a smile on her face. She still doesn't know about the mess you made. You open the refrigerator but it is empty. There is nothing to eat. When Mother was alive, she always cooked lunch. But Parisa either doesn't eat anything, or she makes herself a quick bite to eat. At first, she didn't have the patience to cook twice in one day. And now she doesn't even have the time to do it.

Parisa pours herself a cup of tea and sits down at the kitchen table. She seems to be in a good mood. Her expression is vaguely cheerful. You don't pick up on any of this. You don't care why Parisa would be in a good or bad mood. You only pick up on the signal your stomach sends to your tiny brain, telling you that you are hungry. It hasn't even been two hours since you had lunch at the institution. You pour yourself a cup of tea and sweeten it with three tablespoons of sugar. You take a package of bread out of the freezer to have with feta cheese and walnuts. You ask Parisa what she is making for dinner, but she doesn't answer. She is deep in thought. She doesn't complain about the excessive amount of sugar you put in your tea, or the bread that you waste by tearing off the crusts, or the spoon that you put in your mouth and then back into the container of cheese.

Parisa had gone that day to say goodbye to her Guru. She would always return from seeing her Guru with a sweet aloofness. It was always this way; for a while it seemed she was floating on air in an atmosphere a little more pleasant, relaxed and peaceful. Her steps grew light and her gaze, distant, as if all the Guru's promising words were engraved upon her heart. She was never able to return to her daily routine until she spoke with a couple of her friends, went over the Guru's theories one by one and ultimately memorized the interpretation of them well.

These things are what finished off Babak: those unchangeable priorities – the two meetings at the beginning of every week with her Guru, that later changed to once a week. The semi-private class was held in the Guru's home. She would not allow any other plans to ever interfere with those classes. If she had practice, affirmations to do, yoga or anything else, everything else would have to be postponed until a later time. Neither were guests important to her, nor plans made beforehand or trips reserved from months prior. Babak was annoyed with Parisa, who wasn't taking care of her household or life. Ever since she had started those astrology classes, her life with Babak had fallen aside to Parisa's second priority. She was aloof to everything except the weightless feeling she experienced in her practice. Babak had finally had enough of the Guru's commands and her sweet hours spent interpreting and explaining the charts to her friends. Mother gave Babak the right to be annoyed, especially after their divorce, since her behavior didn't change at all. Parisa's inattentive aloofness hadn't budged. She always shrugged off mother's complaints without care.

You leave the dish of cheese and the bread crusts there on the table. Parisa calmly gives you a little reminder. You don't listen to her and you do not put your teacup and spoon into the sink. When you walk out the door, Parisa sees the dried, yellow betadine residue all over your legs and leaps from her place. You run to your room and lock the door behind you. You need your afternoon nap. Mrs. Smith has put on her negligée and let her hair down to sleep by your side.

You hear Parisa's slippers on the old, parquet flooring as she walks toward the bathroom. You haven't yet settled into your bed, your body heat has not yet warmed the sheets when Parisa begins banging on the door. She is angry and wants to know why you spilled betadine all over the floor and why you have cut up your pants. She wants to know how she is going to find another pair of pants to buy for you with so little time left. She curses you. She says you are big and fat as a bear, eat like a cow and use your brain about as often as a donkey! She is angry because buying clothes for you is extremely hard. She has to buy large-sized pants and then cut at least half the length off of each pant leg. She doesn't have enough time for this. Then she gives you the ultimatum that if you do this again, she won't ever buy clothes for you. You pay no attention to her anger as you toss and turn on your pillow and then finally fall asleep.

You have peace of mind that she knows nothing about today's fight. Of course, they called several times from the institute to tell her about the incident, but the phone was busy. First thing tomorrow morning the school principal, Mr. Vakili will telephone Parisa and wake her from sleep and tell her all about how you started a fight with Mohsen and Fariborz, and hit Fariborz's head against the brick wall in the schoolyard. Parisa will be in a bad mood for having been woken up so early, and won't ask the reason why you fought. Mr. Vakili doesn't know the reason. These things aren't important to the administrators of the institute. The only thing they care about is getting you home in one piece every afternoon, regardless of your emotional needs and sensitivities. And what might have possibly been the reason for the fight. Like today when you couldn't bear the sight of them hanging the poor, tortoise shell kitten. Today at the institute, you fought with them because Mohsen tied the little kitten to the playground bathroom door handle with a yellow string. As soon as Parisa finds out that the reason

73

you cut up your pants and your shirt got dirty was because of a simple fight, she will get back to sleep. Last night she was awake all night organizing her CD's and computer files.

When you wake up in the evening from your afternoon nap, you hear weeping coming from Parisa's room. It seems like a lot of guests are there and everybody is grief-stricken. The door to her room is open, so you go inside. The room is dark. The light from the computer monitor glows on Parisa's face. Her cheeks are wet and she is weeping. When she sees you, she gets up and opens her arms. She hugs you tight, kisses you and cries. You nestle in her arms. Since mother died, it hasn't happened very often that anyone would hug you, let alone tightly. It feels good to you. Parisa sits down and you stand by her chair watching the video of Mother Zari and Father Ali's funeral. Parisa keeps asking what crazy person filmed this event under those circumstances.

Pooya, you aren't in the movie. They didn't take you with them that day. You stayed behind with Mr. Safa. But Parisa is in the movie standing next to the empty graves, along with Aunt Fati, Tooba, Lady Azar, Father Hamid and the men wearing black in the family, crying. One person has gone down into Father's grave and is nodding his head, inculcating the prayer said by the Behesht Zahra Cemetery prayer giver. Parisa is seen in the film crying out loud. She is crying now too. You don't know whether it is because of seeing herself in that state that has upset her so, or because of experiencing the funeral in the film once more. You think she is crying to get attention. For you, crying is a great way to attract the attention and pity of others. You have no clue that Parisa is crying in the film from pain, fear, sadness and now from loneliness, desperation, and not having anyone to turn to. Whenever you get upset, you start a fight. But wherever you look, you find an answer. You know well how to cry. Like every year during Ashura –Tausuaa, or during the nights of Ahiyah. It had been many years since I quit going with Father. But you liked to go with him and sit in the mosque and wail. Your crying would warm up the gathering a lot and would bring those who have forgotten their God to their knees in repentance. It's your favorite pastime, both getting attention and pity. Do you remember that trip to Mashad? What a show you put on! I was so young I didn't know the difference between the walls and those silver grates around the saints' tombs, or the shrine courtyard and the backyard. You still don't know the difference between these things. We were sitting by the Golden chamber while father said his prayers. Mother and Parisa were in the women's section. You looked both ways, and then started watching the people wailing as they prayed to God to grant their prayers. You noticed how they looked at you and how they pointed at you. You realized what to do to attract their attention. You wrapped short, fat fingers around the shiny silver grates and rubbed yourself against the shiny rhombus network that fills the room with the scent of rosewater and stuck one side of your face to it and began crying in desperation. Father interrupted his daily prayer to calm you down. But couldn't overcome the simple-minded masses who were flocking toward you to intercede for them. They were simple-hearted humans who were touched by your crying. They thought you weren't tainted by the world as they were, that you were pure and innocent and therefore closer to God. Your prayers would certainly be granted. They each tore off a remnant of your clothing as a relic to rub over their face and eyes to be granted their prayers. They surrounded you. This frightened you and even though Father wanted to slap your face hard right then and there, when he saw how people looked at you with hope and desperation in their faces, he kept up appearances and took you in your torn up shirt to the exit of the shrine. I was right behind you. I never understood why Father got so mad. I didn't know that you would never understand the meaning of what you did. Innocence has no meaning to you. Whether God exists or not is a concept totally alien to you. And you never pray. Your purity is of another kind. Your purity is a childish instinct, as well as your meanness and ignorance.

The sound of the crying in the movie is starting to disturb you. You're starting to get angry. Parisa realizes this, turns the media player off and turns on the light. No, she didn't want to upset you. No, this is not her way of taking revenge on you. It is just that seeing these images makes her exclaim as she wipes her face and nose, "Who was it that had nothing better to do than to take these videos and how is it that I've never seen them before?" She felt so alone and heartsick. You are the only companion she has these days. You must be patient. Your burden has always been carried by other people. This past year, your burden was carried by Parisa. Calm down a little. Try to understand her. Sit by her. Calm her. Try for once instead of making her cry, to dry her wet cheeks. Burying her loved ones less than forty days apart was too hard for her to bear. Never-ending funerals seem to be a part of our family heritage. The smell of halva from the last funeral has not yet cleared out of the house when the next batch has to be made. Even though, Pooya, you have never set foot in a funeral or graveyard, you love halva at funerals.

Mullah Hassan had barely stepped away from the funeral of his second son when the departure of his only student, Seyed Hashem devastated him even more to the point where he couldn't even rise from his bed for a long time, and was the impetus for him to eventually leave his homeland once more. A while back, he had been expelled from clergy school because of his passion for black magic and his continued study of it. Because he couldn't return to his birthplace, the city of Babol, then known as Barforoosh, he went instead to a small town in the vicinity. It took a long time for him to clear his name. It looked as though he had repented and was spending his time there doing good deeds unto others. He founded a school and taught the village girls and boys the Quran and Golestan, and in the afternoons, he taught their parents lessons in ethics. Little by little he was chosen as the local clergyman in the village shrine and lead the congregational prayers. He was still young. Over time people forgot about his black magic practice and many men recommended their daughters in marriage to him.

Mullah Hassan had been born into a religious family. His grandfather was a clergyman, well-versed in the traditions of the prophet. People in the surrounding towns knew that his prayers were always granted. Never would a day pass when they didn't summon the old man to a person's sickbed. Hassan's mother had made a pact with God that if God granted her a son, she would send him to clergy school so that he would become pious and exalted like his forefathers. Mullah Hassan did not have many memories of his maternal forefathers, for he had lost his mother when he was fifteen years old. He was a mischievous boy without any goals. Before he went to clergy school, he had studied The Principles of Religious Doctrine and Gems of Wisdom under the tutelage of his grandfather. He would study during the day with his grandfather, and in the evenings, he would go up to the rooftop to sit and watch Latifeh, the girl next door, as she washed the dishes or clothes. He hadn't seen her for a few days and heard from his mother that Latifeh had a high fever and was very sick. The physician's diagnosis was Typhus, but the medicines he gave her for it didn't have any effect. They brought a chaplain and an exorcist, but her high fever and delirium would not let up. Hassan took his grandfather's hand and led him to the neighbor's house. They saw how his grandfather laid hands upon the hot, perspiring forehead of this pale and emaciated girl as he recited the Hamd Sura and got up, closed her door and prayed for her there until morning. Latifeh had lost so much hydration during this illness that her skin was now wrinkled and her lips were pasty white. Her sullen face disappointed Hassan, who had imagined her to be much more beautiful than the image he was presently seeing. Latifeh came to an hour after the morning call to prayer and her mother arrived that same day with a basket of fresh, red apples to thank them.

They had sent Mullah Hassan to clergy school in Qom at the age of sixteen. Before that, in addition to the Quran and the traditions of the prophet, he had studied Islamic doctrine, mysticism, interpretation of dreams, and had touched upon numerology. But he never knew how his grandfather was about to predict the future and most importantly, how he healed people. The night his grandfather died, Hassan's uncle Reza had taken on a grave illness. Tuberculosis was claiming his last painful breaths. His father's praying all through the night and reciting the Quran, didn't appear to be working. All these years he had prayed for healings for others, but now his own son was in a sickbed while his prayers weren't being answered. In the middle of the night when Hassan got up to go to the bathroom, he heard his grandfather crying. He was sitting by the fountain facing Mecca, his hands outstretched to the sky. He never forgot the sentence he heard that night and for the rest of his life. He went to sleep every night in wonder and awe of the scene he had seen with his own eyes. His grandfather was looking up to the full moon in the middle of the month of Rajab with his hands outstretched in supplication for God to take his life in place of his son's. Then he stepped into the fountain and performed his ablution. Hassan was watching from afar. He saw his grandfather put on clean clothing, kiss his son on the forehead, and get into bed. The next morning, uncle Reza was awake, his coughing had subsided, and he was asking for something to eat. They kept the news of his father's death a secret from him for a whole week. The night before Reza's healing, his father had gone to bed with a smile on his lips and a glow in his face, and never woke up. Young Hassan was going through difficult times in the absence of his family. He wasn't showing any interest in religious doctrine or principles. He was always looking for books about his grandfather's special ability and ways of foretelling the future. After his grandfather's death, he went through all his books and personal belongings but found nothing. One day on his way back from his office, an old man approached him, took his hand and put a ring into the palm of his hand. There was a prayer engraved on the sacred yellow agate. The old man said that it was a keepsake. He then told Hassan the location of a village outside Qom called Abkhoshan and said that he was to get there by the next day and deliver the keepsake to its owner. Hassan was not able to look into the face of the old man, no matter how he tried. There was something in his face, that wouldn't let anyone look into his face or his eyes - like a two polar opposite magnets. He kept the ring in his hand all night and couldn't fall asleep. He set out for that village as promised before the sun came up. The old man was sitting in the shade of a willow tree at the beginning of the road, waiting for him. The dirt road leading to the village ran along a river, which willows overhung on either side. The river had clear, rushing water and the sound of the water hitting the large rocks along its sides reverberated through the air. The low hills around the village were dry and treeless. The old adobe homes in the village had large gardens. Hassan gave the ring to the old man and walked through the village streets and gardens with him. The village houses were separated by apple and apricot gardens. The climate in the village was mild and the sky was blue. The garden gates and front doors were open. The women had their carpet weaving looms out in the courtyards and were busy weaving prayer rugs, while the children played hide and seek. The chickens and roosters and sheep wandered the streets. The old man took Hassan to a house where they kept the handwritten holy tablet that was believed to be the protection of the village from any kind of evil. As they walked, the old man greeted the village inhabitants and asked them one by one if anyone they knew in the village had ever taken ill or died from unnatural causes or any reason other than old age? And whether any catastrophic event had ever befallen the people of the village? The answers were all negative, from young to old. Then he took Hassan to his house outside the village. Hassan began to reject clergy school from that day on and began to spend many days and nights at the home of his Master. Until the day when he received his father's handwritten letter warning him that if he did not change his ways he would be disowned. Young Hassan had only recently discovered the sweetness of the supernatural sciences. He did not want to abandon his study and therefore did not, until one night when he dreamed of his grandfather crying. When Hassan in his dream asked him why he was crying, he knew that it was because his mother had died of a broken heart. The next day, Hassan set out for Barforoosh. When he arrived, no matter how he wished he could, he didn't have the heart to knock at his father's door. He wandered in the vicinity for forty days, repented and then went to a nearby village to begin a new life. Later on after his marriage, he went to Qom on the pretext of going on pilgrimage. And each time he went, he searched for the village of Abkhoshan. But no one had ever heard of it. No matter how he searched using his memory and navigational skills, he was unable to find it. It seemed like it had been part of a dream or even a nightmare that he had awoken from.

When he married Badri, he trusted that God had forgiven him and accepted his repentance. Badri was a beautiful and pious girl from a poor family. Her parents worked menial jobs for people in the village and prayed to God not to be granted any more bread eaters. Badri's mother had given birth twenty-five times, but only eleven of her offspring reached adulthood. Seyed Mosib, the village grocer, spoke kindly about Badri's personality and her piety in praying right at the appointed times. Hassan had once seen Badri from afar thanks to Seyed Mosib. She was bending over with her slender figure as she swept his shop with water. From that very day, he asked for her hand in marriage. The girth of her braided hair was so thick that you couldn't hold it with two hands. She had blue eyes and red lips with the fragrance of candy. She left Hassan wanting nothing with her housekeeping skills and her kindness. She was like a full moon that shone upon his sins with a forgiving light. His good fortune was complete with the birth of his two sons, Mohammad and Reza who were born nine months apart. When Mohammad and Reza reached the ages of six and seven, their father began homeschooling them. Seyed Hashem who was Seyed Mosib's son and was the same age as Hassan's sons joined them every day for lessons. It was at that time that Badri became pregnant once more. A few months later when the only apple tree in their garden produced fruit for the first and last time, Mahin was born. She was a girl as beautiful as her mother, even though her eyes were not blue, she was fair as moonlight, had blushing cheeks, and golden hair as fragrant as the yellow and red apples growing in their garden. Because of her likeness to her mother, they named her Mahin, like the reflection of the moon. Every week, Badri would wash her daughter's long, sleek, sunny golden hair, comb it and adorn it with the most beautiful ribbons. As close as

Hassan was with his sons and Seyed Hashem, whom he loved as his own son, Badri was busy raising her beautiful daughter, whom every lady in town wanted for marriage to her son. As Seyed Hashem grew older, so did his special interest in Mahin and his tendency to superstition. He had heard things about Mullah Hassan's past and had made him swear to teach him his special knowledge. This was a temptation which Mullah Hassan ultimately failed to overcome and agreed.

Seyed Hashem arrived every day for his lessons and for the hope of seeing Mahin's golden hair shine for just a moment. He was a sharp student who showed a lot of promise, unlike his own sons with whom he was as close as one spirit in two bodies. But his sons preferred going into business and quickly abandoned his studies to work in the bazaar. Seyed Hashem would arrive at Mullah Hassan's chamber every day at nine in the morning. He would sweep the courtyard with water, arrange Mullah Hassan's books, and bring him the best sweets and candies available in his father's shop. He maintained the expected customs and respect. He did whatever was in his power to do for Mullah. Once Mullah Hassan, in the middle of the lesson, mentioned a book entitled, The Book of Instruction in the Elements of the Art of Astrology that he had been searching for many years, but had not been able to find it. Three weeks later, Seyed Hashem brought this book for Mullah Hassan. He had asked his relatives to find it for him at the Tehran Bazaar and send it to him. Together, they delved into reading and learning about astrology according to Abu Reyhan. And because Seyed Hashem was younger and had a more active mind, it turned out that Seyed Hashem read and interpreted the book for Mullah Hassan.

During Ashura in the year that Mullah Hassan's eldest son, Mohammad suffered the ruptured hernia under the Alam and died, spring was almost over and the month of June was hotter than usual, incarnating the desert of Karbala, bringing it to life, giving a vivid picture for the mourners. Reza and Mohammad went to the shrine very early in the morning on the day of Ashura. When Mahin was getting ready to go out and watch the procession with her mother and father, she heard Seyed Hashem on the patio. Before she could call her father, Seyed Hashem gestured for her not to call Mullah Hassan outside. He wanted to speak with Mahin, herself. Mahin put on the black head covering that she had set aside for the Ashura mourning ceremony and went out. Seyed Hashem put a letter into her plump, fair hands and left. Mahin's lips blushed even pinker than they were before. She went into the outhouse where she would not be bothered, to read Seyed Hashem's handwritten letter, in which he confessed his love for her. Right there for fear of her father, Mahin threw Seyed Hashem's letter down the toilet, but entrusted the words to her heart. The whole day passed in a spirit of heartfelt reconciliation as she watched the mourning ceremony of Imam Hossein. When her brother, Mohammad collapsed under the weight of the heavy Alam, Mahin felt like all these events were happening in some strange dream, a nightmare with no end. At least five men fell under the Alam and were injured, and several hours had gone by before the doctors attended to Mohammad. His feeble body could not bear the weight of the Alam nor could his soul stand remaining upon the earth. Mahin who had wanted to tell Badri first and then her father about Seyed Hashem's love for her, decided to wait until the first anniversary of Mohammad's death. It was a dreamy year of seeing Seyed Hashem with sweaty palms, bashful and trembling as he placed his letter into her hands. Seyed Hashem was extremely shy as he came and went from Mullah Hassan's house, for he dreaded the possibility of not seeing love in Mahin's eyes.

Ashura in the following year coincided with the first anniversary of Mohammad's death. Mullah Hassan had forbidden Reza, who was terribly unstrung, from leaving the house that day, as well as Mahin and Badri. He locked them all inside the house. He couldn't stand to see people look upon his family members with pity and was afraid the mourning ceremony for Imam Hossein would revive his family's own grief. But he had to attend. People expected him to participate in the Ashura traditions. Reza wasn't having it. The pain of losing his only brother was too much for him. He got down to the alleyway from the rooftop and ended up in the self-flagellation procession of a group that had come to the shrine from a nearby village. By the time Mullah Hassan was able to reach Reza in the throngs of people, he had been hit by the blow of an amateur in the procession. His head was split open and was on the ground in a pool of blood. The drumming stopped. People in black surrounded Reza's body. A stream of blood trailed from his head over the dirt as curious women gathered around, screaming, but careful not to get their galoshes bloody. Mullah Hassan took off his cloak and wrapped it around Reza's nearly lifeless body. He kissed his son's bloody forehead. He held his son in his arms yelling and invoking Imam Hossein all the way home, not able to hold back the tears streaming down his face. The doctor wrapped up Reza's head and poured pain reliever into his mouth and said he would return that night. Reza was out cold. He wasn't coming to. He was burning with fever and delirious. That night after the physician saw him and told Mullah Hassan that there was nothing more that could be done for him and that he might not survive until morning, Mahin watched her father through her foggy window of her room as he brought a bucket full of water out to the courtyard, outstretched his hands to God and asked Him to take his life in place of Reza's. He begged and cried. He swore on whatever amount of good reputation he and his forefathers may have ever had. He repented of all of his past sins. He asked forgiveness because of Seyed Hashem and the lessons he taught him. Badri was at Reza's bedside with Mahin wailing with each of Reza's heart wrenching moans on the other side of the window. Hassan faced Mecca and performed his ablution with the water in the bucket, then he went into the house, put on fresh clothing and kissed each member of his household, but he couldn't bring himself to leave Reza's side.

By the morning call to prayer, Reza had left the mortal world. Seyed Hashem, who knew what Mahin's answer was that the wedding would have to be delayed for another year, set out on a trip towards Qom to find Abkhoshan, which no person had ever heard of except Mullah Hassan. No matter how long Mullah Hassan waited, Seyed Hashem wasn't returning. After the one year anniversary of Reza's death, Mahin revealed to her father the story of Seyed Hashem's courtship of her. Mullah Hassan was shocked. How could he have been oblivious to his daughter and Seyed Hashem's hidden love for each other? How could he not have seen such an evident and unavoidable event happening right before his eyes? He cried that night until morning with regret for his neglect of his daughter Mahin's exemplary grace and Seyed Hashem's innocence and pure love and the failure of these two coming together in wedlock, which had been his hope and dream. He cried for Seyed Hashem's absence, for the days and lessons that he realized were all for nothing more than his love for Mahin, for the lessons and commandments that Seyed Hashem had learned and now wondered what use they would be to him at his young age.

That night he went to sleep with a broken heart. He didn't rise for the morning prayer. When he opened his eyes, the sun was already up. Badri screamed out loud when she saw Mullah Hassan's face. Mullah Hassan went to the mirror on the mantle and was shocked at what he saw. All of his hair had turned white overnight. He started to say something when suddenly his teeth began to fall out and blood trailed from the sides of his mouth. He passed out from fear. He was bedridden for a while with a fever and wasn't able to talk or eat.

When his condition eventually improved, he took Mahin and Badri's hands and set out for somewhere without a shrine, similar houses or streets or anything that would remind him of his sons or Seyed Hashem.

Five

Nevermind about him. You lean back on the couch in front of the air conditioning vent and let the royal blue scarf fall off your head onto your shoulders. It is hot and you aren't sure how long you'll be left waiting in your overcoat. You unbutton the overcoat to let the air blow over your chest and neck. What if he isn't ready an hour from now? This is what Pooya always does. He waits until you tell him it's time to leave before he begins taking his shower and then he locks the door to his room and makes you wait two hours while he gets ready. He won't answer his door, nor open it. No amount of threatening or yelling at him has any effect.

He's done this before. Do you remember that trip to the north, Parisa? We were all ready to leave right after morning prayers at dawn. You and I were in the car waiting to leave, but Pooya wasn't coming out. We waited until 8 a.m. Finally father broke down Pooya's bedroom door, but he still couldn't win that fight. Pooya was sitting on his bed and wouldn't move. He said he wanted to stay home by himself and that he couldn't stand being around the family. No matter what father did, he was not able to budge his heavy body even one inch. It was only after we had unloaded all our things from the car that Pooya suddenly got into the mood to go on a trip and went and sat down in the car. You know well that there is no way to change him in a situation like that; the more you plead with him the more stubborn he becomes.

You call Aunt Fati on your cell phone and tell her that you're still dealing with Pooya. You know that on days when you're going to see Baba Hamid, he's so excited to see you that he gets up early in the morning. He counts the minutes until you ring the doorbell. This anticipation wears out Tooba Jun and Aunt Fati. Father's day is only a few days away but because you'll be going to Shahmirzad at the end of the week, you planned on going to see them tonight. And that it might be the last year that you will see him on Father's day, he feels anxious in his heart. And it makes you cry at the thought that it is the first Father's day that Dad isn't here. But you still don't think of me. There is no "Man's Day" on the calendar, or "Son's Day" which is what I was. There is only Father's Day, an experience which death took away from me. You remember all the Father's Days you passed through in your life without much thought, without a present for Father or even a "happy Father's Day!" And your opinion still hasn't changed. These occasions that they have recently put on the calendar are to you meaningless, identity-less inventions of consumeristic society. Real affection doesn't need any particular day to be expressed. And you have never been one to tie yourself up with society's conventions. Perhaps this is the first time that an occasion like this has had this much meaning for you.

Time seems to stand still. It's a good time for a cry, and you've cried all your makeup off. You reach into your purse for your makeup bag. You haven't yet taken out your compressed powder compact when Pooya shows up. "L..l.lets ...ggo!" Without taking your eyes off the image of yourself in the compact mirror, you ask in a calm, listless tone with crying still in your voice if Pooya went to the bathroom or not. Pooya answers, "I..d.d.don't have to." You ask is he is sure and Pooya answers, "I..s..s..said I..d.don't have to!" You tell him to sit down for a minute until you finish what you are doing. Pooya doesn't listen to you and walks out to the parking garage. You dial Fati's number on the way out and tell her you're on the way there. While you are there, Fati has to leave the house, otherwise, Pooya might have a fit again if he sees her. You don't know what he sees in Fati that revives mother's memory so much. Their facial features are similar. When they stood next to one another, everybody would be able to tell that they were sisters. But you and I never see that likeness in Aunt Fati and mother, except that both of them were teachers and teachers behave similarly in that they tend to want to teach everybody.

They are always advising others. Mother was more simple and practical in her dress. Aunt Fati took greater care in her appearance. But if Tooba Jun died one day, Parisa, you would remind me of her. Have you seen the pictures of her youth? That black and white photograph they took in the courtyard under the fig tree at Baba Hamid's house? I think she was a newlywed at the time. She had your medium height, slender waist and long hair. You are a little fairer and blonder than her, though. When you were born, you were blond-haired and blue-eyed. Little by little, the color of your eyes turned hazel, and your hair got darker. But you can still see that light newborn hair in the filtered sunlight or lights in the house. Especially after you come out of the shower. Your hair becomes silky and full of light. But Tooba Jun had jet-black hair from the very beginning. Your graceful, slender nose is similar to Tooba Jun's. And your eyes as well. There is something in her eyes that reminds me I've seen the same look in your eyes before. I don't know. Why do people often say that you look like father? Not only in your appearance. It could be in the way you talk, interact, or in your distant gaze – I'm not sure what it is that reminds me of Tooba Jun. But there is something about people like an essence or quality – a special fragrance. Maybe if like you, I understood things like auras and different ethereal bodies and things like that, I could determine your similarities on that level. Maybe Tooba Jun is a Gemini like you, but because we don't know her exact birthdate, it is hard to be sure.

Pooya takes the car keys from you and opens the car door with the key fob. He pretends to sit down at the steering wheel and while talking to himself, he then sits in the passenger's seat. Whatever you do to try to get him to fasten his seatbelt, he won't. He has brought his favorite music with him and you are forced to bear listening to it all the way to Tooba Jun's house. Pooya talks to and laughs with the person he thinks is sitting next to him. You're completely used to all this. You know well that her name is Mrs. Smith and he is talking to her about buying a car. When the music gets to a part that he loves, he starts swinging his hips right there in his seat. He purses his lips. You know he is enjoying himself by his squinty eyes and his smile. You smile too. You don't know that this is the last time you will be going somewhere cheerfully with Pooya. The next time it will be on the way to the institute early next week before leaving for Shahmirzad. The whole way to the institute, you will try to hold back your tears. Right now, it's better to engrave the image in your mind of you and Pooya listening to the music.

You hug Tooba Jun and kiss her cheek. You want to feel her scent for eternity and feel her flabby muscles underneath her long sleeves that are not proper for the season and keep that hug in the muscle memory of your arms forever. She smells like you, Parisa. Don't go searching for any special fragrance in vain. But Baba Hamid smells of the cheap aftershave that he has put on especially for you, after shaving with great difficulty and with Tooba Jun's help. You can't pull yourself out of her arms because you know you may never experience a familiar hug like this again. Your guess is correct. Next year on your first visit back to Iran, you will visit his grave. It is that double grave right next to Maman Zari's that Baba Hamid bought for himself and Tooba Jun last year after Maman Zari died.

Pooya says hello very politely and shakes Baba Hamid's hand. Baba Hamid cannot see very well, only a faint light that reaches his retina, only enough for him to see the shadow of objects right in front of him. And as Tooba walks with great difficulty, you go into the kitchen instead and pour the tea to drink with the cake you bought from Bibi Confectionary on the way there. That was Pooya and my favorite cake. One of those cakes wouldn't last half a day in our house! Fati got dinner ready and left. Wish she was here. It wasn't right for her to have to leave. You wish you hadn't brought Pooya here so she wouldn't have had to leave. But you know that Tooba Jun and Baba Hamid are not physically able to make the trip to visit Pooya at the institute. And they will surely miss him.

Your eyes fall upon a set of silver candlesticks and a matching mirror that you have never seen before, on the cabinet in the corner of the kitchen. The silver set shows off in the modern atmosphere of the home that thanks to Aunt Fati's taste, she has decorated and kept immaculate. You are about to ask about the candlesticks and mirror set when you see Pooya rush into the bathroom. You get up and follow after him. Seeing a yellow trail of urine on the ceramic tiles ruins your mood. You knock at the door to see how he is doing. You say you won't scold him, but he doesn't answer. The sound of the running water can be heard outside the bathroom door. Tooba Jun watches from the other room, but doesn't notice the yellow trail. Before she can get up to go into the kitchen and turn on the stove under the food, you pick up a tissue and wipe up the trail. When Pooya comes out of the bathroom, his pants are soaking wet. It is obvious he had taken them off and washed them in the sink so that you would not find out what he did. You signal to Pooya that you aren't going to yell at him. Then you go and tell Tooba Jun what happened, all except the urine on the floor, because you know how hard it is for them to clean. So it is better for them not to even know about it. This way, the sin for the ritual uncleanliness will be on you, Parisa. Tooba Jun looks in the closet and finds the largest pair of pajama pants with an elastic waistband that she can find. Then she rolls the pant legs up half-way. Pooya looks ridiculous but at least he won't catch a cold. You go and wash the bathroom, rinse off the door and walls, and spray some room fragrance. You wipe the door with antibacterial cleaner. When you're out, Tooba has set the table. Baba Hamid is upset that you went to the trouble of cleaning the bathroom, insisting that they would have done it later. You ingratiate yourself with him. You ask him if he still plays the tar. You see the Yahya brand old Tar that is collecting dust in the corner of the living room. What a futile question considering the condition of his eyes and the uncontrollable shaking in his hands. You stand next to him sheepishly and kiss him on the forehead as you take his wrinkled hands in yours and for the first and last time in your life, you tell him you love him. Baba Hamid kisses you and turns his head the other way, too embarrassed to let you see the tears streaming down his cheeks. You escape into the kitchen so he won't feel on the spot. You throw Pooya's underwear and pants into the wash so they'll be done by the time you have to leave. You will hang them out to dry at home.

Fati has made Ghormeh Sabzi so good that every time you think of her not being there makes it hard for you to eat it without her. Tooba Jun tells you not to forget to take the dried herbs they have dried for you with you when you leave as well as another gift they have for you as a going away present.. You thank her and ask her what it is. Tooba Jun smiles and gestures at the mirror and candlestick set. She says that it is an antique – a keepsake from her mother-in-law. It has been gathering dust in storage for many years. Poor Fati took the set to the bazaar one day to have it professionally polished. It is truly an object of beauty. But it must be very heavy and valuable. They might confiscate it in airport customs as a valuable artifact, and not allow it to be taken out of the country. Neither do you want to risk offending them by not accepting the gift, nor can you resist such a gift. You thank them profusely and give yourself some time until it is time for you to leave to think about whether to take the gift or not. Tooba Jun doesn't let you touch the dinner dishes. She says that she will take care of them later. You pour the tea. This will be the last cup of tea you have together. But Pooya interrupts even this occasion. He is sleepy and you know that if he falls asleep on the couch, you won't be able to move his heavy body and you both will end up staying the night there. You want to stay with them at night. But what about poor Aunt Fati? She can't remain at her friend's house until morning. You get up quickly and say goodbye and pull Pooya to the car. You warn Pooya in the car that if he falls asleep in the car, that he will have to sleep there until morning. Pooya doesn't listen and you have to call Mr. Safa in the middle of the night to help get Pooya from the car into his bed.

You still haven't started the car when your cell phone rings. It's Tooba Jun telling you that you left the dried herbs there as well as the silver mirror and candlestick set. You apologize and promise to come and pick it up before you leave. But you won't do this. It is better to leave the engraved silver mirror and candlestick set for Aunt Fati to look into as she combs her hair every day and puts on her lip liner. It is much too heavy an item to take on this trip, both in the sense of silver weight, as well as in the sense of long forgotten memories attached to it.

Tooba Jun's mother-in-law, Malakeh, who is also Tooba Jun's uncle's wife, has very much wanted to gift the set to her only daughter-in-law for the bridal spread. She said that this mirror and candlestick set is good luck and had been used on the bridal spread of many happy couples has brought blessings, bounty and long, happy marriages to them. But Tooba wouldn't be forced into anything Malakeh wanted for her. Instead of an antique mirror and candlestick set from the Qajar Era that was back in fashion, she wanted a crystal set with red crystal, tulip-shaped candlestick globes. No one from her family had ever had a set like that on her bridal spread. Malakeh, wasn't even able to convince her own daughter Pooran to use the set. Pooran also wanted a set like the one Tooba had bought. There was a strong rivalry between the two cousins who were having weddings and starting their married lives within the short span of two months between each other.

Mostafa and Morteza and their sister Soori all had houses in the same neighborhood. Soori had a house on Goethe street, and the two brothers lived on Iran street. When Jamal was twelve years old and their daughter Jamileh was a toddler, Soori's husband passed away, leaving a large inheritance for them. It was an inheritance that Soori's late husband earned from his investments in the businesses of his brothers-in-law, Mostafa and Morteza. Before Soori's husband died, he had bought Jamal a bicycle. In those days, not many people had bicycles in the neighborhood. And every evening in front of the envious eyes of his peers, Jamal would go stop by Morteza's house to chit chat with his cousin, Hamid. Most of the time, Tooba was there, who was Hamid's sister, Pooran's age. Jamal was taking refuge from the silence and loneliness at home in his uncle's home, and

Tooba from the busyness at home and the constant coming and going of her sisters and their children. Hamid was one year younger than Jamal and was afraid of riding a bike. But even though Tooba was two years younger than Hamid and had a tiny, delicate body, but if the adults would have seen her riding that bicycle, they would have given her a good scolding. She would take Jamal's bicycle and ride around her uncle's courtyard. She rode out to the alleyway and completely enjoyed feeling the wind in her black hair and clothes. Hamid and Jamal watched Tooba apprehensively and starting then, planted the seed of affection for her in their hearts. Pooran, who had a crush on Jamal and was jealous of all the care and attention her brother and cousin were paying Tooba, tattled to her uncle's wife, Matineh on Tooba for riding the bicycle and when Matineh didn't show any interest in Pooran's information gathering because she was so engrossed in other things, Pooran took matters into her own hands. On one balmy evening in June when Jamal was at their house sitting by the fountain with Hamid, she went after bicycle which was leaning against the old fig tree in the garden that was full of ripe figs. Pooran took a heavy duty yarn needle from her mother's sewing box and punctured the back tire. That evening, Tooba arrived at her uncle's house right at the time that Jamal was leaving to go home. That day, thirteen-year-old Tooba had the experience of her first period. She had refused to listen to her mother who begged her to stay home and not go anywhere that day. As Jamal's eyes and mind were on

Tooba's feminine sauntering and the brilliance shown in her fair face framed by her jet-black hair, he sat down on the bicycle with the punctured tire. With the first turn of the pedal, he was thrown off the bike. Jamal fell to the ground, hit his head and split open his forehead. Pooran, who was frightened and sorry for what she had done, quickly called the adults to take Jamal, who was unconscious, to the doctor to treat his wounded head. Tooba being physically thin and wispy, seeing the spilled blood by the garden in the courtyard made her faint. Hamid used the first and last opportunity of all the commotion of the family getting Jamal to the doctor. He picked Tooba up in his arms and brought her inside. Tooba opened her eyes to Hamid's gentle stroking. Pooran was standing in the doorway holding a glass of sugar and water; Hamid jumped when she walked into the room, but she didn't let on that she saw him kiss Tooba.

Pooran never admitted to what she had done, but as time passed, she hated herself for losing Jamal's affection for Tooba that she could see was growing stronger. The days of their adolescence were coming to an end. Love and affection that was forming between them, was starting to shape their futures.

With the passing of time, the closeness between Pooran and Tooba, and the distance between Hamid and Jamal was increasing. Jamal did not show any interest in going into the family business of his mother's brothers. He liked studying. At first he wanted to become a teacher, and then a journalist. He was interested in politics, was a staunch supporter of Mossadegh and nationalizing oil. He would debate for hours with his uncles, whose businesses had taken a hit after Mossadegh came to power. Ultimately, he decided to spend his inheritance from his father for his future, and become a doctor with a specialty so that he could both help people and earn back all the money he had spent for his education.

But Hamid never participated in these political discussions. He spent every morning in his father's booth at the bazaar, and every evening and night with his Yahya brand Tar, Hafez and Khayyam. He had tried many times to compose poetry, but he just didn't have the right words. His hands, his pick and the strings of the Tar were the only tools he had to speak the language of his heart. The more the time passed, the quieter and shyer he became. Whenever Tooba visited them, Hamid would play the Tar and his expression of love for her would reach her ears in the form the music he released throughout the house. And Tooba was in love with Hamid's lyric-less music, his quietness, his shyness and his modesty. Many times she had a mind to ask Hamid to come for her hand in marriage. But she was afraid that she might be misinterpreting the love she thought he was directing toward her in his music.

Tooba stopped by to see Pooran every day. They would spread a rug underneath the fig tree and sit and chat. Pooran would sometimes tell Tooba all about her love for Jamal. But Tooba was afraid to tell her that she was madly in love with Pooran's brother, Hamid. She was afraid that Hamid might not be in love with her the way she imagined, and she didn't want to hear such a bitter fact from Pooran. Hiding all of these secrets, excitement and sweet dreams that Pooran and Tooba shared with one another turned into jealousy, envy and hate when Jamal asked instead for Tooba's hand in marriage. Mostafa and Matineh had given an affirmative answer to Aunt Soori, without so much as asking for Tooba's opinion in the matter. Lace fabric, a ring and a Quran that they had wrapped in a Termeh fabric bundle for Tooba was placed at the back of the cupboard until Mostafa and Reza returned from London when they could hold the wedding ceremony. And Jamal, no longer had to worry about marriage, registered at the London UCL University Medical College and set out for London with his father's brother, Mostafa.

When Jamal and Tooba's engagement was announced, and Jamal left for London, Pooran was extremely heartbroken and holding a grudge against Tooba. In order to restore her sense of self-respect, she accepted the marriage proposal from her next door neighbor, Mahmoud. Ever since Pooran's uncle Mostafa had helped him get started working in the bazaar, Mahmoud had been very successful. After a few years, he was able to open his own fabrics booth and was earning a lot of money. But the prospects for a good future was not the criterion for Pooran's choice; what she was looking for in Mahmoud, is what she had already found in Jamal – that quality in Jamal that Tooba didn't like – a kind of stubbornness, obstinacy, pride, willfulness and temper. Throughout all these years the more indifferent Jamal was indifferent to Pooran's affections, Pooran had become more and more enchanted by him; and the more Tooba resolutely and surely refused Jamal, the more in love Jamal fell with her.

Mahmoud, who had been waiting for an affirmative from Pooran for quite some time, prepared the best gifts to give her at their engagement party. In addition to a fine Quran and a diamond ring, he meticulously chose the best fabrics from his store. He cut them and folded them: a length of botanical design Guipure lace, fabric lining of the same color for her engagement dress, and lace edging, netting, Guipure lace and white satin for her wedding dress, two meters of rust-colored crepe for a skirt suit, pink and white floral-pattern poplin for a prayer chador, handwoven Termeh fabric for a prayer rug and knapsack, and three pairs of shoes the colors of the fabrics from the shoe bazaar. He made arrangements for the tailoring of the dresses with Mr. Mohsen, the best tailor in the bazaar who sewed dresses only for the wives of ambassadors and diplomats, and with whom getting an appointment was difficult to say the least. In addition to all this, he purchased a whole set of cosmetics, perfume and a small, white, leather suitcase to hold all the gifts.

There wasn't much time left until the return of Mostafa and Jamal to Tehran, and the wedding ceremony of Tooba and Jamal, and after that, the wedding ceremony of Pooran and Mahmoud. Tooba and Pooran had both become melancholy and heartbroken after Jamal's departure. They always felt suffocated and would leave the doors and windows open. They would splash cold water on their faces. They perspired so much that they lost weight. Matineh and Malakeh thought these symptoms were just the usual love and anticipation of a fiancée prior to her wedding. Their guess was correct. But their love burned in the flames of hopelessness, anger and helplessness. Tooba stopped going to her uncle's house. She couldn't bear the hateful glances of her cousin, Pooran. She was looking for a way to show Pooran that she was not at fault. And Hamid, who neither was bold enough to show up at his uncle's house, nor to speak with Tooba, drowned himself in his Tar music more than ever before. He was hoping that Tooba would come to their home so he could find a way to tell her how he felt, to finally know whether she felt the same or not. In the hopes that his Tar music would reach Tooba's ears, he moved the platform underneath the fig tree in the courtyard. He would sit there and play his music. Passersby would gather on the other side of the courtyard wall to hear passionate sound of Hamid's Tar, the sound which never reached Tooba's house.

Tooba had passed her uncle's house the evening before her father, Mostafa returned. The alleyway was filled with the heartwarming but melancholy sound of the Tar, and the sweet fragrance of the ripe figs in the tree. Tooba leaned against her uncle's courtyard wall, and stood there listening along with the passersby who were there. Bitter tears began to roll down her cheeks. That night, she was wide awake all night. She had made an important decision that she knew might cause a lot of disgrace, but imagining spending her life with Jamal was too painful to bear. She knew that if she didn't do something that day, for the rest of her life she would see the sad, heartbroken face of Pooran whenever she was alone with Jamal. And she knew that from that moment on, she would feel that the sound of the Tar would be the most painful and sad music in the world to her. And she knew that if she just sat there with her palms in her lap, that she would never forgive herself. She got up at dawn, took out a piece of stationery and a pen, and began to write to Hamid. She wrote very frankly that she had heard his music that day, and that she knew she loved him, and she asked him that if their love was mutual, that they should do something about it before it was too late. She gave the letter to her housekeeper to deliver to Hamid before the sun came up. Hamid cried tears of joy for a whole hour after reading Tooba's letter and the loud sound of his Tar that he played in the quiet stillness of the early morning hours woke everyone up. Hamid begged Malakeh to go right at that moment to his uncle's house to ask for Tooba's hand in marriage, though Malakeh wouldn't give in so easily. She was worried about how Matineh and Mostafa would react, and whether they would think it a disgrace, and most important of all, how her sister-in-law Soori would react. Hamid was finally able to convince his parents by sundown to go to uncle's house. When they arrived, Tooba took matters into her hands, served tea and sat down next to her father. She loved Hamid's secret glances and blushed at the excitement of the event about to unfold. Mostafa presented his brother's family with the souvenirs he had brought back for them. Morteza and Malakeh and Hamid didn't know how to break the silence and put forward the marriage proposal. Tooba felt like she was suffocating, and was getting hopeless. When she got up to go to the kitchen, Hamid blurted out his request to his uncle, asking for Tooba's hand in marriage. Right then, Mostafa took his daughter's hand and sat her back down next to him. He called Matineh to come out from the kitchen and join them. He turned to Tooba and told her that he liked both Jamal and Hamid, but that he would turn over the decision-making to her. He told her to make her decision right there. Tooba felt like she couldn't breathe – that there was no air flow in the room. She didn't dare say anything. But after her father prompting her several times for an answer in front of the bewildered and expectant eyes of her aunt, uncle and mother, she finally softly uttered the word "Hamid." After hearing Tooba's answer, Mostafa went straight to Soori's house and returned the marriage proposal gifts. Soori stopped speaking to both of her brothers that day, and never participated in family gatherings again. And Jamal, who had just returned from abroad with Mostafa and Reza, went straight back to London without as much as a goodbye. He completely cut off relations with his mother's brothers and their families. He even refused to visit Reza when Reza's father Mostafa was spending his final hours in the Royal London Hospital, several months after Tooba and Hamid's wedding. He wasn't willing to come forward as next of kin for his uncle Mostafa at the coroner's office and help send his body back to Tehran.

Hamid and Tooba had their wedding and began their married life without delay on the day when Jamal and Tooba were supposed to get married. The festivities were marvelous: there was Tooba's nice trousseau which included every household item, the pristine home procured by Morteza for his only son, and the extravagant wedding party which flabbergasted everyone. Most impressive of all was Tooba in her wedding gown, her beautiful figure which had recently began to fill out, her long, black hair, and her eyes which sparkled with happiness, causing others to envy her. They placed a platform over the fountain in the courtyard for the wedding party and dance. A singer imitated Ruhangiz and Sultan Khanum, singing and dancing around. Pooran was happy for Tooba and her brother. For the first time in her life, she was able to put aside jealousy and rivalry with her cousin. Pooran dressed herself up nicely. While she wasn't very tall, she had lost a lot of weight recently, and in the silver satin dress made from fabric which came from Mahmoud's shop, her figure looked perfectly proportional. The makeup on her smooth, fair complexion, made her big, brown eyes seem even bigger.

Her long, curly hair fell around her shoulders and the way her body moved to the music the musicians play and the songs of love and union the woman sang amazed everybody, especially Marzi, Mahmoud's mother, who delighted in Pooran's smooth, rhythmical movements. But Pooran's happiness was rooted in her hope that Jamal might seek her out after hearing of Tooba's wedding, and that she too might taste of this happiness that she saw Tooba experiencing.

It was two weeks until Mahmoud and Pooran's wedding. Early one morning, a letter from Jamal arrived at Morteza's house. It was a letter for Hamid, which Pooran had received from the mailman. Nobody was home who was literate to read the letter. It occurred to her to go to Hamid's house and ask Tooba to read the letter. On the way, she remembered the   petition writers in front of the mosque at the spring, and changed her route. The petition writer was a young man who wore glasses and had on an old but tidy, navy pinstriped suit. He read the letter to Pooran. The letter was full of threats and curses leveled at Mostafa and Morteza's families. Pooran listened carefully, and each time she insisted that the petition writer read the letter a second time, a third time, she heard no indication of Jamal's love or even mention of Pooran or request for her hand in marriage. Pooran paid the petition writer five rials each time he read the letter, and each time only made Pooran more hopeless. On the way home, she became disturbed even more as she mulled over the words in her mind over and over again.

She couldn't forget the words and expressions Jamal had used to express his anger and disappointment, like may "your generation be cut off," "you die in anguish," "you wish for it," "you have tragedy befall you," "you see your children's deaths," "you grieve forever," "you become terminally ill," "you lose everything." By the time she reached home, she had a fever. She hid the letter in her purse, wondering whether to tell anyone about it or not. She had heard that if a person doesn't tell anyone about a bad dream, it would never come true. She thought that perhaps if no one ever found out about the letter or its contents, the curses would never come true. Perhaps no one in the family better than Pooran could ever understand how Jamal suffered the pain of unrequited love. That night, she took out the letter and hid it in her bra. On the excuse of going downstairs to get some pickled onions, she took the kerosene lamp down to the basement. Even though Malakeh was sure the pickles were all gone, Pooran told her there was one more bucket left. She took out the letter to burn and destroy in the flame of the lamp. She was afraid that she might be the first victim of this letter full of curses. She was feeling guilty for thinking only about Jamal during her engagement to Mahmoud, while she now knew that Jamal hated her and her family the whole time. The sound of footsteps in the courtyard distracted her for a moment. She dropped the kerosene lamp. Before it hit the ground and smashed into a thousand pieces, the kerosene spilled onto the short, open collar of her floral poplin dress, trailing right over her gold necklace, down the buttons over her stomach and down her midi skirt, leaving a wet, cool feeling on her skin. As soon as Pooran realized what was happening, the lamp hit the ground and she was suddenly in the arms of the burning flames of the angry lover that she had always yearned for. Pooran screamed, louder than she imagined she ever could. All the unspoken words and all the silenced sounds that were pent up inside her after that night were suddenly let loose. By the time Morteza and Malakeh got down the basement steps and saw Pooran in flames, the flames had burned most of her skin and face. By the time Morteza ran for a blanket to put out the fire, half of her face was disfigured.

It wasn't until many years later that anyone found the half-burned letter with the name Jamal written in large letters in the corner of the basement. Later when the house was sold and demolished and rebuilt, the half-burned, barely legible letter was thrown out with the rest of the household rubble.

The first degree burns in her throat and chest damaged her vocal chords and permanently took away her ability to speak. She became fed up with the visits and looks of pity from family. Marzi, Mahmoud's mother didn't come to see her for a whole week. When she finally did show up, she apologized profusely, saying that her daughter took ill with fever and delirium on the same night that Pooran had the accident and has not yet regained consciousness. Pooran did not let Marzi come into her room or see her. She pushed the white suitcase

112

that had once held fabrics that were now dresses and suits, out the door of her room and watched Marzi's relief through the crack in her door, as she left after a few words of small talk, never to be seen again. Even though the burns tormented her, the only consolation she felt after some time, was in giving back Mahmoud's wedding gifts, and dodging a lifetime of unhappiness with him. Nevertheless, she was upset with Marzi, and felt sorry for her mother. It was hard for her mother, Malakeh to put off her daughter's wedding so easily. At that moment, Pooran remembered Jamal's curses. She tried to control herself not to hate Marzi for her unkindness and thoughtlessness. But she couldn't. She was too heartbroken to be able to forgive in spite of her pain.

Razieh's delirium and Pooran's nightmares seemed to go on forever. Pooran saw an infant with flaming fire in its eyes that kept getting bigger and bigger and finally swallowed her up. She knew that it was just a nightmare. A fear of fire had come over her and what tormented her was her inability to scream or wake up. She couldn't tell anybody about her dream. It was no longer possible for her to sit and chat and get things off her chest, like her secret love for Jamal, his hateful letter, and a thousand other unspoken words that she had pent up in her heart. Pooran turned little by little into a silent shadow walking to and fro throughout the house. In her heart, the fire still flamed. The only witness to her existence was the sound of her dress brushing against something in the room, for her footsteps on the carpet were so light that they made no sound at all.

And Razieh found no relief from delirium. They thought there was a spell put on her. Razieh had been asleep that night when Pooran's screams attracted all the neighbors. When Razieh awoke to the sound of Pooran's screams, the room was dark and the family had all run over to help the poor girl. Razieh was so terrified, standing there in the darkness of her room that she wet herself. When her mother finally returned, horrified at what she had seen, she came into the room with a light and found Razieh burning with fever and talking deliriously. The doctor had said that the terror she had experienced that night triggered a mental breakdown and that it would be better to transfer her to a mental hospital. But her parents wouldn't give up on her. They thought she might snap out of it any moment. They brought an exorcist, but it only made her worse. They recited various prayers to undo the spell, but none were efficacious. Razieh would beat herself against the doors and walls and talk in delirium until she would pass out and sleep.

Once he had gotten the wedding gifts back, Mahmoud, without so much as a thought for Pooran, took that same white suitcase and gave it to his other next-door-neighbor, Mehry and invited all friends, acquaintances and neighbors to the wedding, even Pooran and her family. Pooran became very upset upon hearing about Mahmoud's wedding and more insulted for being invited to the wedding ceremony. She couldn't stand it anymore. She was weary of spending a whole life isolated, without anyone to talk to. First she considered using opium. But thought that the blackish tar might get stuck in her narrow, wounded throat and not go down. The night of Mahmoud's wedding, she overcame her fear and went down to the basement with a glass of water. Her mother and father did not attend the wedding; they too were melancholy and went on pilgrimage to the Imam Saleh Shrine in Tajrish on Friday evening. Pooran took the packet of Aluminum phosphide pellets, crushed them into powder with a spoon, and stirred the powder into the water before swallowing it all down with great difficulty. Right there, she put her head down on the cold basement floor. As her head leaned back on the lime floor covering of the basement, right at her last living moment, her eyes fell upon a small, half-burned piece of paper behind the burlap sacks of rice in a dark corner of the basement. As she read it with her last breath, it brought back that nightmare she had. A fiery-eyed infant waved a half-burnt letter in front of Pooran's eyes.

The night of Mahmoud and Mehry's wedding, Razieh's mother had given her a tranquilizer, put her to bed and left her alone in the house. Many months after that night, Razieh went into labor. Her screams were reminiscent of Pooran's screams on the night when fire consumed her body and soul. Razieh's childbirth lasted until morning. The child wasn't able to pass through the birth canal, and she had lost a lot of blood. The midwife didn't know what to do. Marzi had not discovered her daughter's pregnancy until the sixth month. Despite Razieh's restlessness throughout nine months of pregnancy, she never miscarried. Marzi was hoping the child would die in childbirth. Razieh, however, did die in childbirth and her delirium ended. But her newborn came into the world screaming loudly. No one ever knew with whom Razieh had conceived that child on the night of the wedding. Marzi was left with a newborn boy who had fire in his eyes. At first, she thought it was only in her mind. But the other members of the family could see the flicker of fire in the child's eyes too. They entrusted the child to the neighborhood mosque for someone to be found who would care for the child, otherwise they would send it to the orphanage. Less than a week after Razieh's funeral, a young couple who had heard about the situation from one of the members of the mosque, came to pick up the child. When they said goodbye, Marzi asked how she could check on the child in the future. They wrote down an address in Abkhoshan village located outside of Qom and said that they would be taking the child there.

Six

You don't wear jeans. The tightness in the legs bothers you. You have a long drive ahead of you to Behesht Zahra Cemetery. You are more comfortable wearing some Adidas sweat pants and a button up Tricot overcoat. Before leaving, you peek into Pooya's room through the crack in the door. Mr. Safa took Pooya for a good shower and now he is sleeping peacefully, like a baby without a care in the world. He takes deep breaths. Neither does he hear the children playing in the alley, nor does the June afternoon sunlight, shining in on his skin through the seam in the heavy curtains hanging in the window, rouse him from sleep. He is sleeping despite all the commotion, worries and decisions to make, as if he has had no past, and no future is awaiting him. Time stops while he is asleep. You were never sure whether or not Pooya had dreams. Of course, he sometimes woke up in a daze and told you he had had a bad dream. But he wasn't able to tell you what that dream was about.

Parisa, Pooya dreams just like we do, but he remembers his dreams less easily, and they affect him less than they affect us. He isn't like you to become disturbed when they describe unnerving dreams about a worrisome future – like that recurring dream you have had many times after my death: the Chalus Road and the black rocks barking along the embankment. You told your Guru about this dream. You told Tooba Jun. You told your friend Mehrnoosh, who knew how to interpret dreams. Everyone said it was a bad omen. You also gave to charity as a way of warding off any calamity. But the accident didn't take place there. It happened on the flat road from Semnan to Tehran, which is a desert road, without hills or valleys, a road where there is usually not one drop of water to be found, except that night when they were returning to Tehran from visiting Azar Banoo, when an intense downpour rained down upon them. The roads became very slippery. Mother got worried, but father was right. They were half-way home already and turning back to Shahmirzad made no difference with continuing on the road to home. Stopping on the side of the road was dangerous so they slowly continued on their way. He drove carefully. It wasn't only mother and father. There were almost ten other cars colliding on the slippery asphalt. A truck carrying laundry detergent flipped into the oncoming lane, and all the detergent spilled onto the road, foaming in the heavy rain and making the road even more slippery. Mother and Father just had some bad luck. Their car slid three times and spun out, finally hitting a passenger bus in the oncoming lane before coming to a stop.

The rain slowed down the ambulance. Heavy traffic formed on the road to the nearest hospital in Sharif Abad which was a long way away. The impact to their heads was bad, and their spirits didn't have the heart to stay. Their grief was now forty days old and it began to tear away one-by-one at the strings connecting their spirits to their bodies. There was a strange sense of lightness in them, freedom from years of pain, freedom from the grief of the loss of a child. Perhaps if they had had a little more hope, mother, whose injury wasn't quite as severe, might have survived. But it was she who eagerly embraced death in her arms. She put up no fight to try to stay alive. Their grief for my loss was still too fresh for them to desire to fight for life, in light of Pooya's annoying and stubborn behavior and your temporary insensitivity and carelessness during those days when your decision to go abroad had become a certainty. If they had survived, I'm sure by now they would have been wishing they had died in that car accident so as to avoid the pain of separation and distance from their child, tearing them apart inside by watching their only daughter pack her bags and say goodbye.

Parisa, you want to go into Pooya's room and kiss his baby face with its peach fuzz, right where the sun light is shining on it through the bright window. You reconsider. Mr. Safa will come and take care of him. The deeper he sleeps, the more secure you feel. You haven't kissed Pooya very much. You know that soon, the chance you have now to kiss him will be lost forever. But now, the way he is sleeping peacefully like a defenseless pigeon, breaks your heart. He doesn't know that this is the last day he will be resting in his own room. From tomorrow morning on, when you will be leaving Pooya at the institution, he won't sleep well for days. He will barely be able to eat the food there that smells like camphor. He will abide the days and nights without any concept of how long it will take for them to pass, while he waits for someone to take him away from there, back to his own home, his own room, his mother's arms, to the old, wrinkled hands of Baba Hamid that pat him on the shoulder, and even you nagging, Parisa.

Pooya doesn't understand the concept of homesickness, but he still misses all those who have left him and continue to leave him. In his mind, there is no sense of succession of people leaving him; he just understands their absence. He misses the things that he doesn't have anymore: the refrigerator that he could open and take out and eat anything he wanted, your maroon-colored Peugeot 206 that he thought was his own red car and would pretend to drive, my pack of cigarettes that he would steal one from and pretend to smoke. He will miss his own privacy, where he could do whatever he wanted, heedless to anyone else. He will miss having no routine, when he could eat whenever he wished, sleep, take a shower, dance or cry.

The strict hours of serving breakfast, lunch, and dinner and "lights out" at the institute feels to him like being in a prison, and because of his inability to understand the concept of time, seems like an endless fence surrounding him. You know all of this, Parisa, but what can you do about it? It's true and you know it. But didn't you work hard to pull yourself out of all of your own walls and barriers? As if it was an easy task breaking through the bars in that prison of belief that you grew up in, or breaking the idol you created out of mother and father in your mind, or breaking the marital bond that was formed from a mistaken idea of what you thought he was when you married him for all the wrong reasons, and breaking free from your family? No, Parisa. It wasn't easy – all these years of finding yourself and improving yourself. You know what you have to do. No one would ever want or let you sacrifice your whole life to Pooya, who in the end, wouldn't appreciate you or benefit from you. Pooya is a closed circle – a complete dead end. He is an idol representing sacrifice that you must break. He is the last wall separating you from freedom, the last step you must take before your rebirth for your future as the glorious Parisa Khani-Porshokooh!

You're sick of all this. You eject the pop music CD, and put in "Keepsake from a Friend." There is only one week left until you'll be free from all this pollution and traffic. You try to fool yourself by seeing Tehran as an ugly city; by ignoring the beautiful green spaces decorating the city, like along the Hemmat Highway or around the Modaress Freeway that you always imagined looked like the hanging gardens of Babylon. The same way with brightening the bright future ahead of you. Maryam is very happy. She is making a good living by doing astrology chart readings alone. But at the bottom of your heart, you have hope that you will be able to escape marriage as a necessary requisite to having a child, and taste the sweetness of becoming a mother without having to unite with anybody else.

Behesht Zahra is calm and quiet. The silence of the dead seems to push down the voices and swallow them. Walking along beside the old, wooded area full of graves, you reach number 238. There is yellow dirt for as far as the eye can see. All of the graves are now full. On the day they buried me, you were more terrified by the empty, uniform graves they had dug all in rows, than you were by my funeral. You had to step carefully on either side so as not to fall in. My grave is on this side of the plot. Mom and Dad's grave is on the other side. You come first to visit me. The sapling that Mom and Dad planted at my grave has dried up. No one has come to visit me in a long time to water it, or at least ask the grave keepers to take care of the tree. Parisa, how nice that you haven't planted anything at Mom and Dad's grave. You sit down very calmly next to me. You don't say a word. You don't read the Quran. You don't confide in me. Why, my sister? Isn't that my name engraved on the stone, Reza

Khani-Porshokooh? There is no sign of Payman, my nickname. Maybe that's why you don't feel my presence. Ok, that small tear drop that has rolled down your cheek and moistened my dusty grave is enough. There has always been a lot of silence between us, and you don't want to break that tradition and change what we are used to. I understand.

You yourself don't even know why you visit the graveyard. Neither does it soothe your heart, nor do you pray for the dead or read the Quran for them like other people's relatives and children do. You don't even wash the gravestone. It's just a kind of dependence or compulsion. No, you don't feel closer to us. More than remembering us, you remember our funerals. Maybe you need to remember that day and its difficulty, disbelief and heartbreak so you can feel as if a lot of time has passed and you've forgotten the details and therefore it is ok to leave. I'm not being fair, Parisa. I know you miss us. You can't think of anything else to do besides come here to soothe your heart. There is no one in this plot of the cemetery. You get up and try to reach the other side without stepping on the gravestones. The graveyard is like a big notebook full of poems and literary quotes, like Facebook pages; whenever a person finds a nice poem or saying, he shares it with others. Many of the people buried here have never even read a poem before in their whole lives, and here their graves are decorated with Hafez, Saadi and Rumi poems! Their families are the same way. Just like you who searched exhaustively through Golestan and the Divan of Hafez for a gravestone epitaph for Mom and Dad, but because you couldn't find anything, you turned over the choice to Baba Hamid, and he chose some off-the-wall poem that he loved: "Drink! For eternal life is thus. What results from youth is thus."

The new gravestones have photos. What is interesting is that only men's' photos are engraved on them. This is where you see the different treatment of men and women. Even if you reluctantly agree with putting photos on gravestones, you would never agree with why the images of the short lives of these women would be forbidden; women whose only remains are these bones buried underneath the black and white gravestones. Perhaps it isn't forbidden, it is just that families prefer it to be this way.

There is a man squatting near Mom and Dad's grave. He rises to his feet as soon as he sees you. He is tall and probably about Dad's age – of course, if Dad were alive. He wears jeans and a simple white t-shirt. He has nicely groomed salt and pepper hair and is well-shaven. You think he looks handsome. He sees the surprise in your face through his sunglasses. He calls you by your first name and says hello. He says he is an old friend of Mom and Dad, and you stand there looking at him in awe. He doesn't delay and says, "There isn't much time until you will be leaving." He gets straight to the point. He knows you are leaving Iran. He had hoped you would stay and study a course in Black Magic with him. He knows your astrology Guru and tells you that your

Guru isn't teaching you as he should. He proves this to you. He knows your whole chart by heart; your Gemini ascendant and Rahu in your ascendant house and counts and interprets your chart's formations one-by-one. It's like your lips have been sewn shut. You can't even utter one word in answer to him.

He describes to you how your leaving won't be beneficial. You won't be able to make ends meet by working your astrology with your weak technique. He says you will hate being so far away from home and your nightmares won't leave you in peace, but will torment you. He talks about Pooya and how you abandoned him at the institute. You don't want to listen to him anymore when he tells you that you will never have a child, even though you had seen all of this information in your chart before, but were in denial of it. He invites you to visit an address he writes down on a piece of paper and hands it to you. Your lips still feel sewn together. He sees you trying to speak and tells you that it is he who has sewn them together, for now is the time to listen. He says that they don't suggest this to people often. He says that there were people before you who were eager to learn that went this route. He asks for your trust. He points to the chakras of your heart and tells you they don't work well. He says to purify them for them to show you the way. Then, he takes his index finger and shows you your ajna chakra right in the middle of your forehead, and tells you to try to open your third eye, that you don't have much time, and to try to visit him with this eye before you leave. You take the piece of paper in your hands and crumple it up. The point in the middle of your forehead itches. He says goodbye. At the last moment, he takes off his sunglasses and you see a strange look that seems not to be focused on any point, and flames of fire in the pupils of his eyes. You turn around to see where the fire is burning that is reflected in his eyes. But you see nothing but dirt and gravestones all around. When you turn around, he is gone.

You automatically take out your cell phone and call your Guru. There is no reception. You look at the address on the piece of paper; it is somewhere in a village called Abkhoshan near Qom. How familiar this name is to you, but you can't remember where you heard it. In truth, you've never heard it but its name has been resounding in our subconscious for many years. You forget Mom and Dad and start walking toward your car. You look pale. You take out a cigarette and smoke it. You take out a mint from your purse and pop it into your mouth. You feel nauseated and you feel like you can't see very well. But you sit at the wheel anyway, and start driving. You call your Guru again. He doesn't take what you've told him seriously. He says to tear up the piece of paper and throw it away. He doesn't ask anything about the man, nor does he explain anything to you. He just emphasizes that you must destroy the piece of paper on the road coming home and you implement his command to a tee. Your forehead stops itching and you settle down.

Parisa, this was the last chance you had to reach the dharma your chart showed, and from that moment you have forever grown distant from it. You will no longer become a meticulous fortune-teller, a mystic and healer whose every wish would be granted. Your hands will gradually lose their ability to heal by touch. No affirmation or mantra or yoga will calm you at night before you go to sleep. You know this intuitively that your spirit has changed. But later on you forget why and where you were changed. You think Montreal is not a good match for your spirit. You think your conscience is nagging at you. All of this is true, but your restless spirit is because you turned your back on a logical choice on the road to finding your peace. You behaved like a rational woman.

The first time Maman Zari saw Majid, she wasn't able to take him seriously or believe what he told her and when she saw the flames of fire in his eyes, she was terrified and got away from his as fast as she could. One Sunday night at the beginning of June, it was 7 p.m. and Dr. Shariati's talk at the Hosseinieh Ershad was about to begin. She was waiting for Ali to arrive and then they would go inside together. They had become engaged three days earlier but hadn't seen each other since that night. She had butterflies. Ali was supposed to be there a half an hour ago, but there was no sign of him. Of course, Ali was in the habit of always showing up late. Before this, both during their courtship and later when they were engaged, he left her waiting many times. Zari remembered all those times after class when she would wait for him at their meeting spot under the single maple tree on Saadi St. She would wait there a long time and Ali would show up each time with a new book to apologize for his tardiness. Once he gave her "Revolution, the Evolution of Islam" by Jalaluddin Farsi and another time "Islamic Economics" by Imam Mousa Sadr, and best of all, the books of Ayatollah Motahari that Zari loved. But this time she expected something different. She thought that he would be eager to see her on their first encounter after their engagement; so eager that he might even arrive much sooner than usual. But no. It seemed that Ali wasn't going to change.

Zari watched from afar, the members of the Islamic Society, who were all Ali's friends as they entered the Hosseinieh. She was too shy to go forward and ask anything. They had not even told anyone yet that they were engaged. She was very shy. She kept fixing her scarf as she inched forward. Fati would tease her because of the tunic, pants and scarf that she had started wearing lately. But it was these things that had attracted Ali in the first place. Zari started getting nervous when eight o'clock passed. She didn't know what to do. Go home and shock her parents and have Fati laughing at her? Or go to Ali's dorm? Then what would she do? Who would she ask about Ali? Or go into the Hosseinieh? Then how would she get home later? And if things got heated, then what? In the middle of her thoughts about her predicament, she became aware of a suspicious young man wearing bellbottoms and sunglasses and staring at her from afar. He was making her even more unsettled. She didn't know

128

what to do. As Zari took her first step toward home, Majid approached her. He said hello. Zari didn't want to answer him. Majid blocked her in every direction she stepped, and finally said something. He said he knew her name was Zari and that she had recently become engaged, and that his intention was not to harass her. He just wanted to talk to her and needed a moment of her time to tell her something.

He said he was looking for something that was kept by Ali's maternal relatives. He said he had been watching and waiting for Ali to arrive. He had wanted to see Ali here today and tell him about it. He asked Zari to bring it to him. It was a ridiculous request. Zari had only ever seen Ali's father, Shahpour and his stepmother, Azar Banoo on the engagement night. They didn't live in Tehran and she wasn't in contact with them. What Majid was asking of her was nonsensical. He was looking for a handwoven prayer rug that he said Ali's maternal forefathers kept and should have returned to its owner. These things were nonsense to Zari and it was getting late. She had to go home. Majid could tell that she was disturbed. Realizing that he couldn't keep her there any longer, he took off his sunglasses, revealing the flames in his pupils to Zari, who stood there terrified and frozen in her place. He said, in return, he would do anything for her. But Zari was more frightened than ever and took off running.

Zari was so worried, she couldn't sleep at all that night. Neither could she sleep, nor could her parents. She was anxious the whole way to school the next morning. When she reached the entrance to the university, she saw Abbas, Ali's best friend. As soon as Abbas saw Zari, he immediately gave her the news of Ali's arrest without so much as a hello first. Saturday morning, the SAVAK agents had called him outside of the dormitory, arrested him and took him away right there. For Zari, everything went black. She was fighting to stay standing on her limp legs. She went right home to see what could be done. Ali loved Shariati. That's all. He wasn't active politically at all except going to talks at the university and the Hosseinieh Ershad. Of course, the guys at the Islamic Society had a lot of respect for him. University students majoring in history were usually well-informed, and this they could use. He became aware of Zari at one of these talks. It was at the Parviz Khorsand talk sponsored by the Islamic Society at the 18th of Dey Amphitheatre that the police came in and broke up. All of the students rushed toward the exit door. A baton injured Zari's leg and she wasn't able to run. She wasn't able to keep up and was falling under the hordes of people when Ali reached down, helped her to her feet, and got her outside. The police were dispersing as they ran in pursuit of those students who were running away. Zari couldn't walk for a week. Her painful thigh and the blow she took to her leg kept her from leaving the house, but after that she and Ali saw a lot of each other at the student sit-ins held for freeing arrested students, at talks and most importantly, at the all-night sessions at the Hosseinieh Ershad.

When Zari heard about Ali's arrest and immediately went home, she saw that man with the sunglasses waiting for her. Majid wasn't giving up. He was insisting that Zari listen to what he had to say. When he saw that nothing would make her stop and listen to him, he blurted out that he could get her husband out of jail quickly. Zari became even more infuriated. She thought Majid had something to do with Ali's arrest in the first place, but when Majid explained that Ali's freedom was in his interest as well, she calmed down. Zari explained that she didn't know a thing about her husband's family and that she was delighted that her husband's family had nothing to do with her either. Ali even came alone to ask for her hand in marriage. She only saw them once and has no relationship with them. Majid described a lilac-colored, handwoven prayer rug with a floral design to Zari and asked her to look around in Ali's parents' house for it. He had heard that Ali had brought it back to Tehran with him, and that maybe it was actually in Ali's possession. Zari insisted on knowing what the importance of this prayer rug was. Majid answered that there is a prayer sewn in the lining which is believed to heal, and if he read and recited the prayer, the flames of fire in his eyes would no longer appear. Zari felt sorry for Majid. She was in a hurry to get home. She didn't ask Majid how he was going to help free Ali, but she promised that if he got Ali out by tomorrow, she would certainly look for the prayer rug. Majid was elated as he returned to his adoptive father, Seyed Hashem. He told him about what happened, and felt for the first time that the fire in his eyes was subsiding and cooling.

Years ago, after Majid was born, Seyed Hashem married a young, destitute girl in order to adopt him and went to Marzi's house with all the required documents. Marzi and her husband, who were happy to rid themselves of the bastard child of their late daughter, showed no interest in resisting the adoption and very easily delivered into the arms of Seyed Hashem the ten-day-old infant with the fiery eyes that set their hearts afire. After that, Seyed Hashem immediately divorced the girl and moved to a little house located outside of Kashan and began taking care of the boy. He raised him well and with discipline. Seyed Hashem was an estimable and successful sorcerer. They became each other's company and confidante and they spent their days and nights in the discovery of knowledge in supernatural science. They went looking for Talismans and ancient epode in the books, and handled the affairs of the people through prayer writing and seeing into the future. In particular, Majid became an expert palm reader. The only thing that bothered this father and son was the unquenchable flames of fire that drove everyone away.

Seyed Hashem remembered a prayer that Mullah Hassan had told him that he had sewn into his prayer rug, the handwoven one from Abkhoshan. It was the only thing he had ever withheld from Seyed Hashem, the healing words for every illness. Majid had gone to Shahmirzad several times to ask Ali's family about it, but each time they told him that there were no belongings of Mullah Hassan remaining in the house. This time, he had put his hopes in Ali as the key that would solve his problem. Seyed Hashem had told him it would be futile to try to acquire the prayer rug by force; the family itself would have to give him the prayer rug willingly, otherwise the prayer would have no effect. Nothing would come of Majid's plan that he had rehearsed many times in his mind to steal the prayer rug.

The next day in the afternoon, Ali went straight from the jail to Zari's house. Ali had been mistaken for someone else. It was a good night. After gathering together and having the delicious dinner that Tooba had prepared, Zari told Ali all about Majid. At first Ali was shocked, then became angry, and then remembered his purple jasmine-colored, prayer rug and began to ponder. When he got home, he ripped open the lining of his prayer rug but found nothing inside. He wasn't sure how to sew the lining back together. He thought he might give it to Zari, and Tooba could mend it for him. The next day at the university, Ali spread the news all at once by passing out pastries for his release from jail and his engagement to Zari. In the evening, he drove Zari home. Majid was waiting for her in her alley. Seeing the young man with the sunglasses, Ali recognized Majid. Ali asked politely to see Majid's eyes. Then Ali pulled the prayer rug out of his bag. Majid took off his sunglasses. Ali was in awe of the flames in his eyes, and Majid was in awe of seeing the jasmine-colored prayer rug with the torn lining. He was very disappointed. He took the prayer rug from Ali and asked whether there was any other prayer rug this color in his father's home, because he had doubts as to whether the design matched the prayer rug Seyed Hashem had described. But he thanked Ali anyway. Zari asked him what he had done to get Ali released from jail so fast. Majid answered, "I just prayed." He took Ali's hands in his, rubbed Ali's palms and read his future. Even though Ali and Zari didn't take his palm reading seriously, they were happy to hear that their marriage would be a happy one and that they would die together. The incurable disease of their first born was absurd to them and they forgot about it immediately. That their third child would die young was as laughable as a joke to them. The only thing that worried Ali was the impending death of his father.

Majid left and was never seen again. Ali and Zari moved into their new apartment the following year during the New Year holiday. Their days together were sweet as they finished their studies and began looking for work as teachers, which was when Zari became pregnant. She had not earned more than a few months of experience teaching when she had to take leave. She had severe morning sickness and couldn't stand the closed atmosphere of the high school classroom, the pungent smell of the students' perspiration and halitosis. Pooya was born in May the following year. They named him Mohammad on his birth certificate, but they called him Pooya. The infant had tiny eyes, fair skin and sparse golden hair. Pooya never cried at birth. Right then Zari knew that there was something wrong. The child wouldn't take her breast and couldn't nurse. She took the child from doctor to doctor. All they did was check the child's heartbeat, and tell her he was beautiful and healthy. When Zari observed that the child could not yet hold up its head at two months of age, muscles were very flaccid, the child wasn't gaining any weight and never smiled, she left the child with Tooba for a couple of days and buried herself in the books at the college of psychology library and read until she became certain of her hunch that her child was afflicted with Down's syndrome.

This time the doctors weren't able to deny it. The infant had mental retardation, was constantly sick and difficult to cure. The repetitive prescriptions for penicillin caused weakness and loss of appetite in the infant. Even though he did not respond to people until he was eight or nine months old, this child was strangely lovable. It seemed like he went through infancy more slowly, which made him a thousand times cuter. Pooya was so loved by Ali and Zari, that Ali was more easily able to overcome the grief of losing his father.

When Shahpour saw three-month-old Pooya for the first time, he was immediately shocked by the recognition that the child had some mental retardation. He had not touched alcohol since before Mahin's death. That first night that Zari had visited their home for the first time, when he saw Pooya's glass-like eyes that stared disinterestedly at a spot and didn't respond to stimuli, he sent for Arthur, the wine smuggler. He waited all night for the cry of the infant to break the night silence. Early in the morning, when he went to use the outhouse at the back of the garden, he caught his foot on the flower box and fell to the ground, hitting his head. He died right there, not from the blow to his head, but by suffering a stroke brought on by intense fear, too much alcohol and sorrow.

Zari's first trip to Shahmirzad which was supposed to have been for celebrating the infant's birthday, ended up in mourning and lamentation.

Seven

Parisa sits at the kitchen table waiting for you to wake up and join her in there. She hasn't slept all night. Thoughts of her strange encounter with that man at Behesht Zahra yesterday and dreading today's goodbye, have robbed her of sleep. Her eyes are swollen from crying so much and from lack of sleep, and she is barely able to open them. When you were asleep, she packed up your personal belongings, emptied your closet into a suitcase and struggled to pull the suitcase out and get it loaded into the trunk of the car. She has put aside a clean pair of pants and a shirt for you to wear today. She has made a nice breakfast for the last meal you will share together: an omelet and the fresh Barbari bread that Mr. Safa bought this morning and delivered at the front door. Mr. Safa will also be moving today. He has packed up his household belongings and will be returning to Shahmirzad. He hopes that he will be able to rent a small store with the money he has made all these years and make a good living. He thinks any job is more honorable than giving you a shower, even though through these years he has made a lot of money from the Khani-Porshokooh family and he knows that helping you was good deed. Nevertheless, leaving and tearing his heart away from this house and the family with whom he shared their happy and sad memories for twenty years is difficult and heartbreaking.

You open your eyes. Your room is vacant and empty. You get up and go straight into the kitchen. You eat your breakfast without a word under the kind, watchful eyes of Parisa. You never answer anyone while you eat. If someone puts a hand upon your shoulder, you leap at them like a cat and fight with them. You devour your food and cram your cheeks; pieces of chewed egg and tomato leak out of the sides of your mouth with the tea.

Parisa clears the breakfast table. She says you have to go somewhere and tells you to go and get ready. You love to be stubborn. You want to take a shower and you make Parisa yell at you. Your whiskers haven't started to grow yet, and you don't need to shave, so you don't notice the missing shaver. First you have to get your clothes ready. You see only one change of clothes in your closet, get angry and start yelling. But Parisa was ready for this moment. There is no quiver in her voice. She yells so firmly at you, telling you to get dressed and get into the car, that you pull your neck back into your green t-shirt like a turtle and without knowing to say goodbye to your room and your home, you go and get into the car.

There is silence the whole way there. Parisa won't let you turn on the stereo. Later on, she doesn't want any song to remind her of these moments. You ask where you are going a few times, but Parisa doesn't answer. She doesn't know what to say or how to explain it. She hopes that after you get there, everything will be fine. The boarding institute is privately run, and charges Parisa a high annual rate for your room and board. It is equivalent to the rent for a 100 square meter apartment in a middle class neighborhood in Tehran. It is a very neat, clean and tidy place. Parisa looked around a lot until she finally found this place. There are fewer than 50 residents and the institute is decorated more like a family home than an institute. Parisa parks the car behind a half-wall separating the parking area from the yard and tells you to get out. The guard comes to help her and takes the suitcase to the lobby. You still haven't figured out what is going on. Parisa talks with the administrator of the institute, Mr. Molaei. You don't listen to them. You are focused on a soccer game in the back yard that you watch through the ceiling-high window in the lobby.

Parisa goes through her list of last reminders with Mr. Molaei. She pulls you toward herself and tells you to say hello to him. Mr. Molaei warmly says hello and shakes your hand. You smile and are pleased when he tells you what a handsome looking guy you are. This calms Parisa's heart. She hopes that he will treat you the same way in her absence. But, well, it isn't always this way. Sometimes personnel are impatient and rude and are not willing to see you as a handsome guy, my lonely brother. First, you go with Mr. Molaei and Parisa to the institute coffee shop. They bring you ice cream. Parisa wants a cup of coffee. While you eat your ice cream and adapt to your new environment, your private nurse, Mr. Mostafavi takes your bag to your room and unpacks your things for you. He is a young rookie in this profession, and you will soon enjoy a good relationship with one another. He understands you and has a lot of patience and motivation. He is smart and sharp and will do whatever he can in order to climb the promotional ladder faster. So relax and enjoy your chocolate ice cream while your room is made ready. When Mr. Mostafavi is done, he will come after you and together, you will walk back to your room. The hallways are long, like in a hospital. It makes Parisa a little sad. But your room is large and open, with a window out to the yard. You can see the sky and the Birch trees through the narrow spaces between the bars welded to the windows, even though the sky and trees aren't your idea of beauty. Your idea of beauty is mostly found in music, and to some degree, in women. Parisa tried to explain to you that this will be your room from now on, and that Mr. Mostafavi will be like your brother Payman for you. It's ok. Let her explain it however she wants. It doesn't matter to me. Mr. Mostafavi smiles at you and Parisa so that you won't turn on him and start having a fit. They have told Parisa not to say goodbye abruptly. Now that you are on first name terms with Mr. Mostafavi and call him Mehrdad, he is supposed to keep you occupied so that Parisa can slip out of the room when you won't notice.

Mehrdad sits on the bed and tells you to sit down next to him and show him your CD's. He says they have a CD player and that tonight there will be a special party in your honor. He makes all kinds of other promises. You confirm that Mrs. Smith will be there too, right? And Mehrdad smiles and nods affirmatively. You are happy and don't realize that Parisa has left the room. She couldn't help herself and dropped at the end of the hallway, sliding her back down the wall, holding her knees in her arms and sobbing, her head on her knees and her body shaking and trembling. She cannot believe she was able to leave you there and go. She feels like a mother abandoning her newborn in order to have a better life for herself. She is at a fork in the road, asking herself whether this was self-interest at play or self-sacrifice? Was it for her better life or the better life of her child? At this moment, it is just the pain of separation that she feels with her whole being. You cannot hear the sound of her crying. The walls here are soundproof. But Mr. Molaei sees her over the closed-circuit camera and goes to her.

Mr. Molaei takes Parisa back to his office and brings her some water with sugar dissolved in it. He tries to calm her by making scintillating promises, by giving her examples of other people who had left their loved ones there. He said it was the best thing to do, that it was in Pooya's own best interest. But the storm in Parisa's heart was the kind you will feel waiting to go home, a destructive kind that will not be stilled. Parisa calms down a little and again starts reminding about your idiosyncrasies, everything she can think of, even Mrs. Smith. Mr. Molaei writes every word down with precision in your file. Parisa called the institute five times that night to ask about how you are doing. And each time she would hear the same answer, "He's doing perfectly! Don't worry about a thing!"

The moment you realize Parisa is gone and start yelling and screaming for her, Mehrdad gets you ready to go to the restaurant for lunch. There, you meet the other permanent guests of the institute. You meet Mehdi who also has Down's Syndrome, with whom you become best friends; you meet Milad, who gradually became mentally disabled due to a severe injury and who always steals everybody's belongings; you meet Payam, who has autism; and each one of these people becomes a member of your new family. But seeing them makes you angry. Accepting to live with all of these people, all at once, is intolerable for you. Mehrdad understands this. He carries your dinner tray and you go back to your room together. You love Barberry Rice with Chicken, but you eat it with displeasure. It has a strange flavor that you have never tasted before. It is the flavor of camphor. Mehrdad slips a tranquilizer into your fruit juice so that you will sleep peacefully in the afternoon, as you get used to being there. If Parisa knew about this, heads would roll! But there is no one who will reveal these professional secrets to

Parisa. It's all the better that she doesn't know about it. She can't do anything about it. At least this way she won't blame and punish herself so much.

When you wake up, you see that Mehrdad has laid out your suit. He tells you to put it on, and come with him to the meeting hall. They're throwing you a party. And like a tamed horse, you listen. He praises you and tells you that you look just like a groom. You take out your red tie from the drawer they stuffed your clothes into, and Mehrdad ties it for you. The meeting hall is full of boys and men just like you, with low intellect, weak memory, and unbeautiful and lonely. Everyone dances to the rhythm that uncle Keyvan plays on the keyboard. It is a happy moment. And you join them. With your hand on Mrs. Smith's hip, you dance and twirl. Mehrdad is happy to see that your ice is starting to melt. Mr. Molaei comes into the meeting hall and says, "Well done!" with a lot of emphasis, which makes him even more hopeful. Then they bring in the two-layered cake especially in your honor, Pooya. Haven't you always wished for such a night? Everyone claps for you. Mrs. Smith claps for you and blows you a kiss. And the dancing starts again, although this time it is the knife dance. At this moment, you are simply happy. You have forgotten everything: Parisa and home, the past and the future, time and place. You laugh and wink at Mrs. Smith who has come in her wedding dress.

At the end of the night, Mehrdad uses the prior technique to guarantee your sleep until morning. The next morning when he comes to your room, he sees that you have gotten dressed, packed your things, and are waiting to be taken home. Mehrdad's work has just begun. He explains that the bus driver, Mr. Habibi will come to pick you up and take you to the vocational school and bring you back in the afternoon. But for a while, you go through your ritual every day. Any time of day or night, you might pack up your things to go home. You may walk out to the main entrance of the institute with a plastic bag filled with your belongings and tell the guard, who watches so that no one sets foot outside the institute, that you are waiting for a taxi, or for Parisa, and several times you have even mentioned my name. You say that Payman is coming after me! But no. It will be awhile before anyone from the realm of the dead comes for you. You will get used to this. On weekdays, as soon as you come back from the vocational school and have a short nap, you realize it is already night time. On the weekends, it is a little depressing, but tolerable because of the weekend parties. After a while, Aunt Fati comes to visit you, and her visits don't set you off. You actually like to see her and you don't even want her to leave. After a few months, she takes you home for the holiday; a holiday that you rub her nose in and make her regret.

You don't see Parisa until next year when she comes back to Iran for a visit. She is going on a two-day trip tomorrow, and after that she will only have time to pack. On the last night of her trip, she will stop by to visit you on her way to the airport. It is not even 10 p.m. yet when they tell her you are asleep. Mr. Mostafavi having used his forbidden technique on you, nervously says that you exerted yourself a lot today, are very tired and are sleeping soundly. Parisa wants to see you anyway, but they don't allow it. She starts yelling and screaming and still cursing, gets into the car. She makes Aunt Fati promise to go to the institute tomorrow to see how you are. On her first telephone call after reaching Montreal, she asks about you. Until next year when she sees you again, that place in her heart that was torn out cannot be filled for even one moment, for her having had to leave without saying goodbye to you.

And I too, left without saying goodbye. That morning I was supposed to go to the office and come home that evening, but that day instead of coming home, I was transferred to the hospital, and then to Behesht Zahra. You had left early that morning. Parisa was still sleeping. Mom and Dad were probably at the vegetable market. That ugly, brown roller cart that we usually keep next to the shoe rack wasn't there. The kettle was on, and there was fresh Sangak bread on the kitchen table. The fragrance of tea and hot bread permeated through the house. I was late as always. I was relieved that I hadn't wet my bed the night before. I didn't make my bed. I didn't take a shower. I didn't shave. I just threw on my clothes in a rush and left the house. I took to my grave regret for missing that last morning breakfast.

In those last months it wasn't only the nightmares that I was fed up with. The recurrence of my childhood bedwetting was troubling me. I was ashamed, and this embarrassment prevented me from telling Mom about it. I had told Dad, and we were planning to make an appointment with Dr. Mohaghi, the urologist whose office was in the vicinity of Pasdaran. Dad said that the problem was likely related to my kidneys or bladder. I was embarrassed when he told me that I had wet the bed until the age of ten. And as much as I racked my brain for memories of it, I could not remember those wet nights or mornings. Dad said that was because they didn't want me to suffer emotionally by confronting me with the fact. Fear of waking up on a wet mattress deprived me of sleep. I didn't dare take a sleeping pill or tranquilizer. I had read on the internet that one reason for adult bedwetting is extremely deep sleep.

Parisa had witnessed my sleepless nights several times. Once when I went at three in the morning to smoke a cigarette out the kitchen window, she suggested that I have a drink, and that it would help me relax and sleep easily. She knew that recommending yoga or mantras wouldn't do me any good. But it wasn't only that I was afraid of the sin of drinking and breaking Mom and Dad's hearts, I simply refrained from drinking anything at night in general, even water. Getting to sleep so late every night made me wake up late too and get to work late. This stress itself kept me up at night. I would constantly watch the clock to see how much time I had left to sleep before 7:45 in the morning. I thought of using adult diapers. I tried it, too. Before I went to bed, I stood before the

146

mirror in the bathroom and struggled to get them on. With one hand I would hold the back, and with the other hand, I would try to peel the adhesive strip and fix them in place. They made my pajamas bulge. I was careful for no one to see me like that, and would get myself back to my bedroom quickly. I felt terrible about it. I couldn't stand it. That morning, I put the diaper into a black plastic bag and took it straight out to the dumpster in the alley. I set the package of remaining diapers next to the big dumpster and tossed the black, plastic bag into the dumpster. I kept watching to make sure that none of the neighbors saw me. I felt like someone trying to get rid of a body. The best solution was putting plastic underneath me. I used disposable tablecloths for this. The best kind had a paper lining against a layer of plastic. These were usually also wider and had nicer designs. After my death, Mom was as surprised to see the various designs in my collection of disposable tablecloth rolls in my closet, as Dad was to find my package of cigarettes in my desk drawer.

It wasn't only the night bedwetting that troubled me, but the nightmares that came before it that frustrated me. In these nightmares, I saw all the members of the family wearing clothes made of white netting, sitting around a table, with stark facial makeup: Mom, Dad, Parisa, Tooba Jun... all wearing different-colored wigs and blue and purple lipstick. Even Baba Hamid was wearing a wedding gown like the women, with his long nails polished orange, and his makeup looked like that of prostitutes. I was the groom and brought tea for everyone.

It was a sumptuous occasion. There were others there besides the people I knew, but their clothing and makeup wasn't vulgar. Their dress was old-fashioned, like in the movies during the Shah's era. The men wore suits and ties, and the women wore midi dresses in the style of those days. I saw them in black and white or in sepia, exactly like the pictures in Tooba Jun's photo albums. I didn't know any of them, but they all seemed to know me. They smiled and waved and wanted me to serve them tea. Up to this point, the dream wasn't that bad, except for the strange feelings I had. But all of a sudden, flames of fire took over everything. I was in the middle and the flames were quickly reaching my feet, going up my legs and spreading out through my fingers and up my neck to my face. My whole body was trembling from the pain, and I would wake up in panic. I could tell from the cool wetness on my thighs that it was a nightmare and I was still alive.

The urologist probably wouldn't be able to do anything for me. The source of my bedwetting was nerves; it was psychological and rooted in my subconscious. My dreams revealed a death lurking and waiting for the right time to take me. The beginning of it is still in my Facebook friend requests, Dr. Jamal Behroozi. Well, this name meant nothing to me. His profile had no photo. The "About Me" part in his profile gave no information about him. Why should I accept his friend request? I was thinking about his friend request the whole night. I had no mutual friends with him except

Parisa. I never accepted friend requests from people whose profiles were blank. I saw no reason for it. But I couldn't quiet the sound of his name reverberating in my head. I couldn't understand why this name was occupying my thoughts so much. I was wide awake until the morning call to prayer. I had never experienced a sleepless night before. I was frustrated and couldn't relax about the issue, no matter how I tried. That same night, when I finally fell asleep, the nightmares began for the first time and I wet my bed at the age of 27!

Parisa had spoken with Dr. Jamal. He had sent Aunt Fati a friend request, but she never checked her Facebook. He had found me and Parisa in her friends list. Parisa found out that Jamal was Baba Hamid's father's sister's son, and she shared everything she knew about the details of our family history throughout the years. Once she called Tooba Jun and told her about it, but Tooba Jun said nothing and gave Jamal the right to inquire about the family after so many years. She thought that perhaps Jamal had forgiven Hamid after all these years. My mind was full of questions. When Parisa told her that Jamal was going to be coming to Tehran, she became happy, though she didn't let on. Parisa gave our telephone number and street address to Jamal. Tooba Jun asked Parisa to give him her address and get a telephone number from him. But Jamal was no longer online and had not seen Parisa's message. He set out for Tehran on the next flight out.

Parisa never said anything to Mom and Dad or to me about Jamal. She only told Tooba Jun, and then she

149

forgot about it like she forgets about many other things, like her appointment with the orthopedic surgeon, or picking up her clothes from the tailor's or taking her medicines on time, and the whereabouts of her wallet. This time, Fati didn't know about it in order to remind her. The day Jamal arrived in Tehran, he gave our address to the airport taxi driver. He was carrying a big tote instead of a suitcase, with two changes of clothes, personal care items, documents and money. All of these he put into a big, Samsonite tote with wheels. He wasn't planning on staying long, a week at the most. He was in the hopes that Dad would find him a good place so he could stay longer. He did not tell his sister, Jamileh, who lived in another state in the U.S. that he was coming to Iran. He wanted to surprise Tooba and Hamid. He saw a way before him, similar to a sweet temptation, for releasing a burden he carried alone in exile for many years. He wanted to go back to the old house and neighborhood on Iran St., like that scene at the end of the movie "Citizen Kane" where Kane finds his childhood sleigh; he could find his childhood bicycle. The bike that had taught him many things and brought him fame in the neighborhood and put a scar on his face as a keepsake that was now as wrinkled as the lines on his forehead. He wanted to go to Pooran's grave, whose heart he knew he had broken. At first, he felt good ignoring Pooran and never asking about her. He was happy taking revenge on Hamid and Uncle Morteza by breaking her heart. But later when he heard the news of her heartbreaking death, he felt sorry. He realized then that he had loved Pooran all along and never knew it. He wanted to go to the bazaar, Darband, Tajrish, and the Caspian Sea. Maybe buy a small villa in Motel Ghoo province and live out the rest of his life there; ask Tooba and Hamid to come visit him and sit with Hamid and play backgammon, sit together by the urn and smoke a cigarette. He had completely forgotten the letter he had sent to Hamid's father many years ago.

He had decided many times before to close his office and go to Boston to live near his sister Jamileh and her family but he couldn't stand her strict German husband, the older he got, the more cranky and persnickety he became. He didn't have the patience for Jamileh's grandchildren as they weren't able to speak a word of Farsi. He didn't feel at all like they had the same blood running through their veins. He thought they were spoiled, mischievous and rude just like other American teenagers, like those shameless, empty-headed, numbskulls that will never get anywhere in life. Like those teenagers who listen to senseless music and read worthless books, someone like me, in love with western music and their best-selling novels!

When Jamal exited the airport and surveyed Tehran's new appearance in awe, he realized he wouldn't be able to tolerate it for even a week. There wasn't much of a difference with his situation in the U.S. But in Tehran, there was pollution everywhere. It was noisy, overpopulated, smoky, crowded, and stressful. The city seemed to exude exhaustion. Tehran's face had aged, as had his own. Like his own image that he could barely recognize in the mirror, he could barely recognize Tehran. And it was futile anyway. The feeling of exile in one's own country is a lot harder to swallow than in a foreign country. He pulled the address out of the pocket of the big Samsonite tote and handed it to the airport taxi driver.

Right then, I turned off my computer and got up from my desk at work. I walked down to the IT office to get my flash memory drive from Parvaneh and say goodbye. Parvaneh was upset. After our year-long relationship that the whole office had found out about, she was expecting me to take it a step further. My problem was not Parvaneh. It was my own nightly bedwetting that I didn't know how to solve. Mom chalked up my constant, secret sheet-washing to my youth. The problem definitely wasn't Parvaneh. She was both beautiful and kind. I loved talking to her. But I had to solve my problem first before I could propose to her, otherwise she would have been stuck washing my sheets for the rest of her life and I would forever feel ashamed and worthless.

But Parvaneh was not having any of my excuses. For her to have to wait for my financial situation to improve, find a small apartment to buy...that day we started arguing about these things. That evening, when it was time to say goodbye, she started acting ridiculous, giving me the cold shoulder and getting upset. She was acting just like any other co-worker, cold and dry. She indifferently said, "Good evening," and I left. At least I had that chance to say goodbye to her. Two days later at my funeral, she cried. She pitied herself. I was happy for her that the consolation of the heartbreak she was going through was escaping a lifetime of married life with a husband who wet the bed. But Parvaneh kept savoring the sweetness of her self-pity. The less attention Mom and Parisa paid her, the more our colleague, Mrs. Mojabi's mother and sister surrounded her. Parvaneh would weep and they would try to calm her down. They would splash water on her forehead and face, she would faint, they would pick her up, and she would act like the heartbroken heroine in tragic drama movies. She created a kind of Romeo and Juliet out of us. She played the role of a beloved whose lover had died in a terrible, terrifying battle. While I might have been terrible, I was killed in the battle of my own incompetence.

Parvaneh was acting so disagreeable when we were saying goodbye, that I started to feel the same way. My eyes squinted, and my eyebrows knit together as I sneered back at her. I stopped and got out of the taxi when I got to the main road. I took a shortcut through the green space at the end of the street and reached the alley. I saw how two young men got off a motorcycle, walked toward an old man standing at our door and attacked him. The old man struggled and held tightly to his Samsonite tote. He tried to resist but it was already too late. One of the motorcyclers pulled out a switchblade knife. I ran over to him and was fighting to defend him, a futile defense that was very soon ended with several stabbings and their escape on the motorcycle. I saw that the old man had fallen to the ground with three stab wounds. He died right there. I only had one laceration in my thigh but I was losing a lot of blood. I struggled to get to my feet and ring the doorbell.

Of course, I didn't die from the knife wound. They got me to Khatamolambia Hospital quickly and I was immediately taken into surgery. The surgery went well. The doctor immediately gave the good news of my survival to Mom, Dad and Parisa, who were very nervously waiting in the waiting room. The danger was over. But that night after the nurse sent Mom and Dad home saying that no one would be permitted inside the CCU and remaining there was not going to do anyone any good, insisting they leave, go home and get some rest, my heart stopped. The nurses all gathered around me immediately, gave me a shock and an injection, and then they called the doctor in. There weren't only nurses there. The whole family was there, except you, Pooya. They were all there with those awful clothes and stark makeup that I had seen in my nightmares. They pulled up chairs all around my bed: Mom, Dad, Parisa and Aunt Fati cried nonstop. The nurses danced and passed out candy to everyone. Once in a while, they would put a smooth and shiny plate on my chest to make my body move, maybe dance. I wasn't able to move. I wanted to raise my head to see their faces. And I wanted to see the faces of my family members in clothes that looked like costumes, and the faces of those strangers in clothes from those old Behrooz Vosoughi films.

A young woman with black curly hair got up from her chair and came over to me. She told me to stay calm. She smiled at me. She had on a floral poplin dress and golden pendant necklace. She had full eyebrows and delicate lips. She told me she was Pooran, Dad's aunt. And as she smiled, I saw flames of fire coming up her skirt, leaping up her back and chest, and crawling into her face and up above. Her face withered in pain as she screamed. The flames reached me too. The hospital bed was on fire. The nurses had fled. I wanted to get up and save myself, but my legs wouldn't move. I was nailed to the flaming bed. The heart monitor showed a flat line and was buzzing. There was chaos there. I don't know whether it was because of Pooran's scream, the buzzing machine or the flames that were engulfing everything, that brought hordes of nurses and doctors bursting into the room. The room was crowded. Between the people sitting around the bed in the chairs, and the flames everywhere, they forced their way near to me. The doctor came near me with a syringe in hand. The nurse, who had covered her whole body, even her face, put the pads on my chest to give me another shock. They had come to put out the fire burning inside me. And they did it.

I opened my eyes again. The room was still crowded. An old woman with white eyes walked to and fro in the room, and was speaking in delirium. Tooba Jun had become a young woman again. Her belly was large. She held the old woman's hand. Someone yelled, "Sit Matineh down! Can't you see she's not well?" I tried hard to raise myself up to see where the man's voice was coming from, but I wasn't able to. He came himself to my bedside. He was wearing a white hat and his beard and hair were white. He hadn't a tooth in his mouth! But his serene demeanor was pleasant. He said his name was Mullah Hassan, my great grandfather. He told me not to worry. It wasn't long before a young woman with golden braids took Mullah Hassan's hand and sat him down. She asked him to say the Hamd prayer. I had a strange impulse to take Mahin in my arms and hold her, and see if she had the scent of Dad or Azar Banoo. I smelled alcohol. Shahpour was standing there laughing out loud. He caught his foot on the foot of the bed and fell down.

Sitting between his father and his uncle Mostafa, Baba Hamid was reading the Quran. He took out a half burned piece of paper from between the pages of the Quran and stood up. He gestured to the unknown old man and said, "Jamal." Jamal was dead. His corpse was sprawled out on the floor next to my bed. Mostafa got up to go into the next room to check on his son, Reza. He was saying that something was caught between the branches of the pine tree. Baba Hamid gave the piece of paper to Parisa. The sound of gunshots could be heard coming from the next room. Matineh was delirious again and wanted to get up and start walking. Tooba stopped her. Matineh was crying glass after glass of tears. Parisa passed the piece of paper around until it reached Pooran's hands. Pooran came and stood above me again. She was holding a newborn. This time, the flames were shooting from the eyes of the newborn and engulfed Pooran in the fire. The fire had not yet spread to my bed, when Pooran screamed again and with the sound of the flat line from the cardio monitor, the nurses filled the room again.

The room was empty. Silent. I saw Parisa standing beside my bed. Her back was bent over. Her face looked worn from the burden she carried on her shoulders. Mom and Dad were standing by the door. Light was coming into the room, right through the door behind them. Mom wasn't crying anymore. She said that it was the end, and that she and Dad would be joining me very soon. Parisa was in such pain that she couldn't stand up straight. You weren't there. Not in any of it. I missed you. I missed you Pooya, more than anyone. I wanted to say goodbye. The sound of tumult came from the other side of the door to my room. A lot of people were waiting in my room. The hospital alarm sounded. The hospital was on fire. I could hear people running down the halls. It was probably patients and hospital personnel escaping the fire. They ran toward the emergency stairwells and swarmed the exit doors. The flames had reached the CCU. I was starting to burn. The nurses were burning and so were the doctors. Mom and Dad were gone. Parisa was burning in the flames with her back bent over.

It was futile. I wasn't coming back. Whether an aneurysm or a stroke after surgery, whatever it was, the way back to life had been closed off in one of my veins. The old unknown man had not died from the knife wound. The coroner determined that fear had caused his heart attack. Before he had even experienced the first stab wound, his heart had already stopped. There were no documents on his person. They were all inside the tote that was stolen. No one came to claim his body. A few months after Parisa went abroad, a woman by the name of Jamileh Behroozi set out from the U.S. for Tehran to find her missing brother. After searching all the hospitals, mental hospitals and jails in both the U.S. and Iran, she came to the Tehran coroner's office. They compared the photo of the unidentified man who was killed with a photo Jamileh showed them, and they gave her the address of his brother, plot number 238, next to the grave of Reza Khani-Porshokooh.

When the unknown, elderly man had died, Mom and Dad undertook his burial expenses for the blessing of my soul.

Eight

You close the trunk of the car. It is full of the things you want to donate in Shahmirzad: old dishes, books, a computer, clothes and bedding. Your mind is not at ease about Pooya, but nothing can be done about it. We're not just talking about a couple of days here. You have to let him stay there and get used to his new home. You've got a three-hour trip ahead of you. The Tehran portion is hard, from Afsarieh until the end of Pak Dasht both the air quality and the scenery is bad. Then when you get to the wide plains that run from the south and end at the desert, and to the north as well are plains for as far as the eye can see. If you had the map of Iran before you, you could see how the Tehran-Semnan route follows along the most northern border of the plains. This route was a part of the Silk Road many years ago, and the ruins of ancient Caravanserais were scattered along the way.

One year on the way back, we stopped along the road at one of these Caravanserais and had some tea. You wouldn't let it go, Parisa. You took photos at the old ruins of the one-story Caravanserai building until the camera's battery wore out. You were saying that there was a strange energy there. Even though there was rubbish, trash and used syringes scattered about the ruins indicated the type of people that passed through the Caravanserai, like the Cultural Heritage Foundation that doesn't give a damn about such places so far from the city.

Once on the way back we stopped at the Dehnamak Village. It was first and last time Babak ever came with us. He nagged so much! He didn't understand what you saw in the adobe walls with the red bougainvillea spilling over them that you would spend so much time wandering through the vacant, uninhabited alleys. The sun was hot and you were warm from the wine of the beauty of the natural, untouched village that had a different kind of life flowing through it. A life made of serenity and anticipation. You still have that photo that you took with that village woman. She brought us cool water to drink. You pulled that photo out of the album so you could take it with you to Montreal. The old woman was squinting in the sunlight but your eyes were hidden behind your sunglasses. She was kind but complained about her sons who went to the city and left her there alone. You loved her loose, white, floral poplin village dress. I took the photo. Babak had taken refuge in the air-conditioned car. He was really fed up and argued with you all the way back to Tehran about your "sentimental" behavior, as he called it.

Right before Semnan, you turn onto the highway headed north. You have to pass Mahdi Shahr before reaching Shahmirzad. These two towns are so close they almost seem like one. The mountains in Mahdi Shahr have a strange majesty about them, despite their drought conditions and dried grasses. Just to think that one time long ago, beyond these very mountains with their steep slopes, bandits like Asghar Yaghi would lie in wait to turn the pleasure of travelers into nightmares, makes the mountain scenery seem frightening and mysterious. They have built a road that leads to the Shahmirzad Cave, and put up a sign that says, "The Mahdi Shahr Cave." You think they may as well have written "Sangesar." That would have been better. In front of the dirt road that leads up the mountain, underneath the sign, you brake and squint to see the dirt path up to the cave better. The dirt path can be seen from there. Here and there, they have built steps so the tourists can get up to the cave more easily. This time, there won't be time to visit, but you decide to go see the cave sometime, to see whether it is the same cave that the bandits hid inside or not. But it isn't, Parisa. The cave you're thinking of is actually behind this mountain. Perhaps there might be a way into that mountain through this cave. The route is hard to pass and they haven't discovered it yet, because no one knows it's even there. And when it is discovered, they won't know whether it is really that cave or not. The treasures inside of it that were the fruits of years of highway robbery have been removed over the years by the members of Asghar Yaghi's gang.

It isn't yet noon when you reach town. Three streets before the main city square, you turn right. You pass several alleys and streets until you reach the dirt down by the river. The villa that construction was started on last year is now ready. It is chic, new construction. You don't understand of what use is a three-story villa with 3200 square foot floors! You love Shahmirzad for its free energy, its separation from pollution, metal and cement. Azar Banoo's house is on the other side of the river. You have to park right there in front of the new villa overlooking the river, and walk to the other side.

You don't carry in your belongings, just your handbag. Later on, you'll have Manege's son, Agha Akbar come and empty the trunk. You grimace seeing the new metal bridge they have built. What's wrong with it? At least you can get to the other side easily. Don't you remember how hard it was to pass over this river? We either had to hop across the large tree stumps and rocks to get to the other side, or carefully make our way across the wobbly boards of wood the locals put there for passing. Either our feet got wet or our shoes muddy. But I agree, the metal bridge with the cover painted dark green, detracts from the untouched, natural scenery. It looks out of place next to the turbulent river which they have not yet contained with cement on either side, and the herds of cattle that are busy grazing on the other side, and the single walnut and almonds trees that have sprung up haphazardly on the riverbanks.

It's not a long way to get to the other side. When you pass the first garden row, you see Azar Banoo sitting on a stool, waiting for you outside the light-blue garden gate under the cool shade of a walnut tree. When she sees you, she gets up and walks toward you. Manege calls from inside the garden, "Madame, be careful not to fall down!" But Azar Banoo is so happy to see you, she's practically flying! She abandons her cane and throws her whole weight into your arms. You kiss her. You smell her. It is strange how much she smells like Dad. She smells like the soil after the rain. She smells like the leaves of the walnut tree. You hold her arm and help her back into the garden. You pass the old fountain that they have rebuilt with cement on your way to the porch. Inside the fountain, they have used a tasteless, cheap blue paint. You wonder what was wrong with the old turquoise tile that they would choose such a bad color of blue? Manege Khanum who is sitting there cutting up a watermelon, says hello. You sit down beside her on the cool porch. In front of you, the many leaves on the apricot trees obstructs the view of the stone garden wall at the other side of the garden. You look up at the sky above you. The sky is so blue that the painted blue fountain no longer looks fake to you.

You tell Azar Banoo about Pooya and the good institute you have found for him. She talks about her leg aches and back pain. You tell her about packing up the household items and storing them all in boxes. Azar Banoo talks about her inability to perform household tasks anymore and complains about Manege who doesn't take care of things properly. You tell her about your plans to go to Canada. Azar Banoo confides in you about her homesickness and her loneliness as well as her fear of exile. You have experienced homesickness and loneliness, but you don't yet know anything about exile. Azar Banoo talks about the first days when she came to this house, sixty or seventy years ago. She herself isn't quite sure. Was she thirteen or fourteen years old then? She doesn't know how old she was at the time. These things aren't what she remembers. She only remembers that she felt exiled. Her grandfather sent her out of Sefioun, a village near Shahmirzad to work as a maid for Shahpour. She experienced exile then. It was hard for her. That morning, taking care of the house, sweeping and washing, helping with the cooking, washing dishes and laundry, bedding and clothing in that fountain that they have now built a cement enclosure around it, painted it and installed a hot and cold water faucet. Back then, the water was cold. They filled the fountain with a water pump. All of this was done under the unkind supervision of Nosrat, Shahpour's mother.

The only kindness Azar Banoo saw was from Mahin. Mahin felt sorry for her. She helped Azar Banoo sometimes. She procured warm clothes and socks for her for the cold, desert nights in Shahmirzad. Once the cards changed and the arrangement was for the pre-teen adolescent Azar Banoo to be married to Shahpour. Mahin became very upset and spent her days and nights at her father, Mullah Hassan's house, who wasn't well. Shahpour knew nothing of any *thing* or person, except those things and people who were dearest to him. His mother was always busy harassing the maids and devising schemes for her imaginary grandchild. Azar never forgot those long nights when she had to tolerate Shahpour's stench until morning. She tells you about it, Parisa. She tells you that she is still a virgin, an old maid that was deprived of all the hopes and dreams that normal women have such as a happy marriage, becoming a mother, being loved and loving others. You see the moisture of tears in her eyes. You take her old, wrinkled hand in yours and kiss it. You both get up. Azar Banoo goes into the kitchen to serve lunch and you go to the bathroom.

They turned the old-fashioned bathroom at the back of the garden into a storage shed. The rooms in the house are built in a line, side by side. The most eastern room in the house is the kitchen, next to which they built a full bathroom and shower. The door to the bathroom opens from the kitchen. The faucet drips. You wash your face and turn the faucet off, trying to get the dripping to stop. It's no use. You know that if you tell Azar Banoo about it, it will only cause her to nag Agha Akbar and Manege more. When you come out, you see Manege setting the little table in the kitchen with the grimy, sticky plastic table cloth.

Azar Banoo has made her special Shahmirzad Tahchin in your honor. She has arranged lamb meat layered in herb rice with potato slices and carrots around the sides of the pot. She serves the dish with apricot pickles. Enjoy your meal, my dear sister! You won't find anything this delicious again. You will yearn for this flavorful dish many days and nights in Montreal and try to replicate her Sabzi Polou dish for yourself. But the meat won't taste this flavorful, nor will the herbs be as fragrant, nor will the rice be the pure Iranian rice that Azar Banoo steams for you. The next time you go to Iran and visit Azar Banoo, you will find that several months have passed since she had a stroke and the stroke took away her sense of smell and taste. And so her Sabzi Polou is tasteless and without enough salt. So eat, Parisa. For this is the last time you will have such a meal.

Azar Banoo makes your bed ready in the guest room. First you call the institute and ask how Pooya is doing. Then you put on something more comfortable and lie down on the bed. The sheets smell like soap, like the scent of baby clothes. You guess she washes them with laundry soap, without fabric softener. The fragrance of walnut leaves and sunshine that dried the sheets in the garden is a scent that is euphoric for you. You aren't sure whether this euphoria comes from the fragrance of the sheets or the abundance of oxygen without pollution, particulates and noise. You are so exhausted from the three hour drive, your lack of sleep, and the many things you had to do to get prepared in these last days prior to your trip that you fall into such a deep, dreamless sleep. Your body is heavy and limp and when you wake up, you can't believe that you've been asleep for four hours! Azar Banoo's evening tea has boiled, so she steams a new pot for you. She tells you to wash up and come into her room. She wants to give you a gift that she has wanted to give you for a long time, but was waiting for the right time. She stresses that she has prepared the walnuts, almonds and the apricots for your trip. And she has for you another keepsake that she was afraid would end up as a donation to the mosque Hosseinieh. It was more valuable to her than for just anybody to have possession of it.

She pulls it out of a tapestry bundle and hands it to you. You feel it with your fingers, the purple velvet, the old, prayer rug and you examine it with your fingers. It is soft and delicate and diffuses the scent of jasmine flowers into the air. You run your hand softly over the weft and weave of the prayer rug with its miniature bird and flower design. Azar Banoo tells you that it was a keepsake of Mahin. It came from her trousseau. A young man was looking for this prayer rug many years ago. He wore sunglasses and each time he begged and pleaded to see the prayer rug, but Azar Banoo never admitted to having it in her possession. She tells you all about how Shahpour used to stay up all night. Mahin was always worried that her prayers would not be accepted if offered inside a home where wine was imbibed. She tried to offer her prayers mostly at the mosque, standing behind her father, Mullah Hassan. But it wasn't always possible. Azar tells you about how one night, she saw Mahin at her prayer rug, as she recited the names of God on her beads, this very velvet prayer rug you hold in your hands, rose two feet up in the air and floated. Azar didn't say anything about it to Mahin that night. She watched the prayer rug rise several nights after that. With the first Allah-o-Akbar of the prayer, the prayer rug slowly rose up, and with the last Salam, it slowly came down to the ground. When Mahin complained about Shahpour and her unanswered prayers, Azar Banoo told her not to worry, that practically speaking, she wasn't actually praying in Shahpour's house, as her prayer rug wasn't touching the floor there. Mahin blushed in surprise when she heard that her prayer rug had risen off the floor. After that, her prayer rug never rose during her prayers again.

Nevertheless, this prayer rug is a keepsake for Azar Banoo which reminded her of the purity and kindness of Mahin's bright spirit. She doesn't want this prayer rug to end up in the wrong hands. You pass your hand the distance of three fingers over the prayer rug, scanning the energy of the delicate, handwoven fabric and you find it has the similar energy of Saturn and Jupiter, the holiest conjunction of planets. You pull Azar Banoo into your arms and kiss her as tears roll down your cheeks. This was the best gift you have ever received. You hope you are able to use it for more effective practices, do your yoga on it, mediate on it or perform Reiki on yourself on it. First you put it carefully into a clean plastic bag, and then into your leather purse. You are curious to know more about Mahin. Azar Banoo has a lot to tell you; things you wouldn't have been able to bear to hear before now. You wouldn't have understood these things. Parisa, because your ascendant lord is Mercury and the energy of Mars bubbles within you, wisdom and patience are hard for you to attain.

Azar Banoo takes the tray of tea out to the patio. You join her and sit down next to her. The springtime breeze diffuses the fragrance of the cardamom tea through the air and caresses your nose. She points to the newly painted fountain in front of the patio. She says that Mahin performed her last ritual ablution in that fountain, in June many years ago. Azar had not seen it, because she was in a sick bed at the time, only a few breaths away from certain death. It was a disease similar to cholera. If it had been cholera, she would have died sooner. The diagnosis was something like cholera. But cholera was contagious, and this disease only affected Azar. Azar in her sick bed could only think of little Ali whom she loved like the son she never had. The thought of death to her only meant separation from Mahin and Ali. She wanted to see him grow up, grow tall and fill out in his youth, and then get married and have his first child. But death was standing at her bedroom door, wearing a white collar; lingering there, leaning against the doorframe, neither coming inside, nor going away. Azar could see it. Several times she tried calling to it, but death was facing the other way. Azar couldn't see its face. She wanted to see what her death looked like, but it wasn't speaking to her. What it was looking at was more interesting than Azar Banoo's pallid face.

Death was watching Mahin, who was facing Mecca that late night. With her palms raised to the heavens, she prayed. She plead with God for the sake of truth; she entreated God through all the names of Allah and the names of all the _prophets and the great men of God, for the sake of the pure souls of her forefathers and the heart of her toddler child, she asked God to take her life instead of Azar Banoo's. She was always afraid of drowning in the banality of material life. She was waiting for a divine test so that she could lose her mortal belongings and be free, purified and washed of her sins. She wanted to take a meaningful step towards God. Azar was young. She had never tasted the sweetness of life, except the sweetness of Mahin's son, Ali and Mahin, who was like a sister to her. Mahin missed her mother and father and mourned for them. She was frustrated with her cold, loveless marriage to Shahpour. Little Ali looked so much like her father. Up until now, he had grown up in Azar's arms. He was so small, he would never miss his mother. There was no difference to him between Azar and Mahin. Azar was everything and every person to Mahin. She didn't know how she would ever get through each dead day without Azar. Who would she confide in? Life without Azar was like death to her. Death that was waiting in doubt at Azar's door. When Mahin put on her pure clothing and sat down at her purple velvet prayer rug and spoke her Amens, death drifted away from Azar and appeared before Mahin. Maliheh had seen everything. So did Nehmat, who in complete disbelief, encountered Mahin's lifeless body the next morning.

You don't believe it, Parisa. These memories have amazed you. You had never heard these things before. You had always thought Mahin died young in the cholera outbreak and that was why Azar Banoo raised Baba Ali.

Azar Banoo is crying. You put your hand on her shoulder to calm her. She says that tonight is the anniversary of Mahin's death, a night that should have been the anniversary of her own death. She knows that if it was she who had died, no one would mark this night. You are eager to know more. Your repetitive questions tire Azar Banoo but she answers them. She tells you everything, from the day she set foot inside that household, about Shahpour's mother's harassment of her, about Mahin's kindness that she took refuge in every night and slept in her arms, and about searching the garden for the talisman. You had heard all these stories before, Parisa. But now it seems like the first time you are hearing them. Azar Banoo's words have a sense of transcendence in them, it is like they all tingle eternally in your brain. They seem to spread under your feet and take you by the hand and raise you up. You jump involuntarily in place. Azar Banoo looks curiously at you. Your face is flushed and the effervescence of the energy on your forehead creates aura around your face, like an image that has been blurred so it won't be seen well.

You get up and ask her where that mulberry tree is; the tree they dug up years ago that dried up and died when they were looking for the talisman. A small flower bed of herbs was planted in its place. The basil has not sprouted yet but there is a lot of mint. You look over everything carefully and begin to spin with your arms outstretched at your sides, you close your eyes and spin. With each rotation, you raise your arms up and lower them down again. Then you stop. Azar Banoo is leaning on her cane as she watches you. You move toward the garden wall gate. You run your hand over each one of the apricot trees growing beside the wall. You feel their coarse trunks with your hand, stroke their lower leaves and smell them. You are giddy. You distance yourself from the wall again and start that movement. You turn the palms of your hands downward and spin as you focus on that round metal token that you feel. Once again, you feel its energy over by the wall, as Azar Banoo watches your movements in awe. You step toward the wall.

You see that half of the walnut tree in the alley overhangs the garden wall and casts a pleasant shadow over the garden gate during the hottest time of the day. You ask Azar Banoo when this wall was built. She doesn't remember. You ask her whether the walnut tree outside the gate used to be on the inside of the garden wall. She says it was. She says there wasn't even an alley here once, and that when she first arrived, they moved the wall back so that they could make an alley. You ask the age of the walnut tree. She says it's very old, that it must be one hundred years old, but it doesn't produce any fruit and the crows won't nest in it.

You run out of the garden gate, without a scarf or shawl, in your jeans and short-sleeved t-shirt. You circle around the walnut tree as you run your fingers over its leaves. Then you squat down next to it and put your hand on the dirt at the foot of the tree. Suddenly you leap. Azar Banoo is so worried, she has come outside the garden gate to see what you are doing. You run inside and grab your overcoat and shawl, then turn toward the storage shed, putting on your overcoat and shawl as you walk. Azar Banoo doesn't know what is going on. You don't answer her. You just ask her to call Agha Akbar to help you.

Azar Banoo goes inside. She dials Agha Akbar's house, which is one street up. That worry in her eyes transfers into her voice, and causes Akbar Agha to drop what he is doing and come quickly. When he gets there, he sees a very pale Azar Banoo at the gate waiting for him, and you struggling to dig up the dirt around the walnut tree. Akbar Agha takes the shovel from your hands as you slowly straighten up. He begins to dig, and after several shovels of dirt, he asks you what you are looking for. Have you found a treasure? You answer very matter-of-factly that you are looking for a talisman, a round, metal token about 10 by 10 centimeters in size. Akbar Agha smirks as he continues digging. After a few more shovels, he uncovers a copper token with the dirt he has dug up. Azar Banoo peeks over to see what you have found. Akbar Agha's eyes are bulging and his legs are limp. He is barely able to swallow. You brush the dirt off of the token with your hand and without saying a word, you go inside. Akbar Agha puts back the dirt he has dug up and fills in the hole under the walnut tree. While you wash off the token you have found, Akbar Agha puts the shovel back in its place, before going to call Manege.

You show the round token to Azar Banoo. You ask whether this was the talisman they were looking for all these years. In the middle of the copper token, there is a circle with a blurry image of two people in it. There are tiny Arabic letters around the edge of the token, and strange geometric shapes and numbers have been carved in a spiral around it. Deciphering the random numbers placed side by side is not your mission. And you, yourself know this. While you telephone your Guru, Azar Banoo lies down on the floor. Manege, having just arrived, helps her and sits her against the wall, puts a pillow behind her back and she stretches out her legs. She brings Azar some sugar water, as she watches you out of her left eye with that round token in your hand. Your Guru says to just bring it to Tehran. He has to see it in order to know how to break the spell. He asks you how you found it. You say through concentration. You focused on feeling the energy of the token under the dirt and you went to it. You hear praise in his tone and feel a sweet sense of pride in your heart. You try to squelch that sense. Pride is the most destructive quality in a mystic. You put the copper token into your handbag and go over to calm Azar Banoo. The sound of the magpies resounds in the courtyard. Azar

Banoo points at the tree. There are four or five of them in there. They are flying around the tree and cawing on the branches, and then they circle the tree and land on it again. Their cawing doesn't stop.

Azar Banoo goes back inside. She lies down until evening. She's not feeling well. You want to take her to a doctor, but she won't come. Before sunset, Agha Akbar and Manege come and unload your things from the car. You prepare dinner. You break some farm eggs into a skillet and grate some tomato over it. You chop several sprigs of mint that you have picked from the garden, and throw them into the skillet. It's going to be a good omelet, especially when you add the Persian hogweed that Manege picked at the riverside and dried herself. Agha Akbar appears right before dinner, and he has brought you some of Shahmirzad's own freshly baked specialty bread called Tanbalak. You make a mental note to remember to stop on your way out of town tomorrow and buy some to take with you. The omelet aside, that bread is delicious enough for you to eat all by itself! Azar Banoo isn't hungry. She tells you she never eats dinner, but you make her a bite anyway. You cajole her into taking a bite or two. She looks pallid and has no energy. You ask her again to tell you about the past, about Mahin and about Shahpour, but you see that she isn't in the mood right now.

She goes to sleep early that night. You take your package of cigarettes, wrap a blanket around you and go out to the patio to sit under the starry sky. Ever since you and Babak broke up, you don't need to hide your smoking any more. You think about Pooya, yourself, and Mahin. Mahin and Azar were considered "rival wives" and yet look how they sacrificed for one another! And you abandon your disabled brother and leave! You kick yourself and berate yourself for about a half an hour until your logic finally kicks in and your start justifying, explaining, and remembering the moments you experienced in life with Pooya, with his stubbornness and annoying behaviors. But you are awash in self-remorse and self-forgiveness, when you hear Azar Banoo crying. You quickly go to her. She is sitting there crying. There are no tears on her wrinkled face, but finding the talisman it seems has opened an old wound. She feels deep emotional pain and cries in anguish. She has the right to. You try to console her, but you can't bring back all the lost years. You both know that there is nothing left to gain. You get a chlordiazepoxide tablet out of your purse and give one to her and calm her with your kisses and caresses, until she goes to sleep.

You find refuge on the patio in the desert silence and your cigarette. This time, you kick yourself for getting into Azar Banoo's business. Maybe it would have been better not to have unearthed the talisman. Her life has already been wasted. What good was finding it and breaking the spell now? Except that it leaves the old woman feeling even more alone and aggrieved. Your Guru always warned you about these kinds of things. Who listens? Besides, this talisman might have been put there recently. It might even be a joke. You yourself don't even believe that all the bad luck and misfortune of the Khani-Porshokooh family was because of this round, metal token! Meaning all of this misfortune, my death and Mom and Dad's death! No it isn't true. If it were true, then you'd never see any misfortune ever again, sadness, death, separation... No, my dear sister. This isn't the end of your woes. They will continue. Your guilty conscience for leaving Pooya will torment you. The sadness of exile will make you restless for home. You will suffer many a broken heart in love. And worst of all, your flimsy beliefs that you have begun to destroy and bring under question. It isn't your fault, Parisa. This was Azar's destiny from the very beginning, from the moment of her birth with a damned birth ascendant, but this rationale is no consolation to you. You shouldn't have done this, and now it's too late for realizing such a mistake.

You fall asleep right there, under the starry sky, under the decorated ceiling of planets, zodiac signs and stars. You sleep without dreams or nightmares. You fill your lungs with pure desert air. When you wake in the morning, your nose is congested, but you don't worry. The sharp noon sunshine will expel the cold from your body. You take Azar Banoo to the Abshar Restaurant and have kabab together. Then you walk together in the natural beauty of the town's alleys and streets. Azar Banoo isn't able to walk much, so she sits down on a tree stump blocking one of the lanes. You take a selfie together there on the tree stump with her in her mustard-colored overcoat and black scarf, leaning on her cane. You share this photo on Facebook three years later after hearing the news of her death and you receive many likes. The comments of condolences are so numerous that you don't have the patience to read them all.

On your way home, you go see the bread baker, Javad Agha. You watch how he makes dough out of pure wheat flour, and rolls them into flatbreads, sprinkles powdered walnuts and turmeric and ginger and puts them into the oven. You buy Tanbalak and sweet bread for yourself, Pooya and for Tooba and Fati Jun. Azar Banoo has sent walnuts and apricots with you to give to them. When you say goodbye, she cries again. She kisses you and tells you to drive carefully. You promise not to drive fast, and to call her as soon as you get there. You don't let her walk you out to the car. You say goodbye to her underneath the old walnut tree. The Magpies have started cawing again since dawn this morning. You look up and see them. They won't settle down on the tree or leave it alone. They circle it and land on its branches. Your leather handbag is on your shoulder, and your heavy plastic bag full of souvenirs is in your hand. You walk along the side of the green bridge and pause there, looking back to commit the view to memory and take one last picture. The plastic bag full of souvenirs suddenly rips and bursts open. As you leap to try to keep the walnuts and apricots from spilling out, your leather handbag falls off your shoulder and down into the river.

You step into the water with your tennis shoes on, and fetch back your handbag.

As you step out of the river with your wet shoes and purse, you notice the handwoven purple velvet prayer rug floating down the river away from you.

About the Author

Zoha Kazemi was born in Tehran, Iran. She moved to London at the age of ten and returned to Iran after six years. She studied Material Engineering and worked as a Quality Assurance Officer in Oil and Gas Companies.

She has always had a deep affinity for literature. She published several fiction translations in well-known literary magazines and wrote flash fiction. She continued her graduate studies in English Literature and started on her first novel in her native Persian, <"Beginning of the Cold Season,"> which was published in 2011. This novel is currently being adapted for an Iranian feature film entitled, <"The Cold Season."> Zoha Kazemi published her flash fiction collection in Persian entitled, <"Put Your Shoes in Order"> the following year.

She stopped her Engineering profession to become a full time writer and literary critic. In 2013, she published two novels in Persian entitled, <"Sin Shin"> and <"Year of the Tree"> as well as writing numerous book reviews and articles for major Iranian papers. <"Year of the Tree"> was well received and praised by the literary circle in Iran and is her first work translated into English by Caroline Croskery. Her latest Persian novel, <"Has Someone Died Here?"> was published in 2015 and her newest novel <"Pine Dead"> is to be published in Persian in 2016. She has also started writing a series of adolescent novels for her daughter. The first book of <"The Vegi-people"> pre-teen series was published in 2016. She lives in Tehran with her husband, daughter and her three Persian cats.

About the Translator

Caroline Croskery has been especially devoted to the Persian culture for many years. She was born in the United States and moved to Iran at the age of twenty-one. She holds a Bachelor's Degree from the University of California at Los Angeles in Iranian Studies where she graduated with honors. Her career has involved three fields of specialization: Language Teaching, Translation and Interpretation and Voiceover Acting.

During her thirteen years living in Iran, she taught English and she translated and dubbed Iranian feature films into English. After returning to live in the United States, she began a career as a court interpreter and translator of books from Persian into English. She is also an accomplished voiceover talent, and currently continues her voiceover career in both English and Persian.

Other titles translated and narrated by Caroline Croskery are:

(2013) *We Are All Sunflowers*, by Erfan Nazarahari

(2013) *Democracy or Democrazy*, by Seyed Mehdi Shojaee

(2014) *The Water Urn*, by Houshang Moradi Kermani

(2014) *In the Twinkling of an Eye*, by Seyed Mehdi Shojaee

(2015) *Stillness in a Storm*, a Collection of Poetry in Persian and English by Saeid Ramezani

(2015) *A Sweet Jam*, by Houshang Moradi Kermani

(2015) *A Vital Killing: A Collection of Short Stories from the Iran-Iraq War*, by Ahmad Dehghan

(2016) *You're No Stranger Here*, an Autobiography by Houshang Moradi Kermani

(2016) *Sidewalk in the Clouds,* a Collection of Poetry by Afshin Yadollahi

Made in the USA
Columbia, SC
16 August 2017